I0619111

HIS SILKEN SEDUCTION

Book 4 of Aikenhead Honours Series

Joanna Maitland

Ben Dexter—wounded spy, abandoned,
a baron in disguise.
In the enemy's bed.

Joanna Maitland Titles

REGENCY HISTORICALS

~Unsuitable Matches Series~
A Penniless Prospect
Marrying the Major
Rake's Reward

~Feuding Families Series~
My Lady Angel
The Solway Bride
Star Crossed at Twilight

~The Aikenhead Honours~
His Cavalry Lady
His Reluctant Mistress
His Forbidden Liaison
His Silken Seduction

~Individual Stories~
The Duke and the Dubious Damsel
The Mystery Mistletoe Bride
A Regency Invitation
[with Nicola Cornick & Elizabeth Rolls]

OTHER JOANNA MAITLAND STORIES
Lady in Lace ~ Regency Timeslip Romance
To a Blissful Christmas Reunion ~ Timeslip Romance
I, Vampire ~ Romance with Bite
[In Libertà Books anthology: *Beach Hut Surprise*]

WRITING AS KC ABBOTT
All Cats Are Grey ~ dystopian thriller
Viper Venom ~ short story collection

HIS SILKEN SEDUCTION

Aikenhead Honours Series, Book 4

Joanna Maitland

Published by Joanna Maitland Independent, 2025

ᴶMᵢ

Published by Joanna Maitland Independent in 2025
LibertaBooks.com/joanna
His Silken Seduction
~Aikenhead Honours Book 4~
revised edition
originally published by Harlequin Mills & Boon Ltd in 2009
by arrangement with Harlequin Books S.A.

Cover Design and Interior Formatting: Joanna Maitland
Cover Images:
© Joanna Maitland;
© Adobe Stock / Jonathan Stutz, yuriyzhuravov

Chapter One

France, March 1815

THEY WERE COMING FOR HIM.

They had appeared out of nowhere. Five of them. And they had knives.

Ben started to run. What choice did he have? He was alone. No…no, Jack was about somewhere. Where? Ben couldn't see him, but he must be—

No time to think about that. It didn't matter anyway. Two against five was very poor odds, especially when the two were unarmed and the five were not. It was every man for himself.

Run, you idiot. The voice in his head was insistent. *Faster. If they catch you, you're dead meat.*

Ben put on a spurt. He could do this. He could

He must.

He was almost out of the old port area. Only another few yards to the end of the quay. There must be safety up ahead. Somewhere. Somewhere less dangerous. With civilised people. If only he could—

Pain ripped through him.

Then—only then—he heard the report. A shot. One of those blackguards had shot him. And he was falling. Falling…

His last thought was to wonder why the ball had hit him before he had even heard the shot.

And then he was floating. Surrounded by shifting dark mists that rolled and twisted into fantastical patterns and shapes. Bringing with them strange, sun-drenched scents.

Am I dead? He dragged in a desperately needed breath. And discovered how much it hurt. *If it hurts, I can't be dead, can I?*

He sucked in another breath. And a blinding light burst through the pain. He remembered. If he was injured, how could they continue with their mission? Their mission for Wellington was vital. Nothing else mattered. Nothing. He groaned out the precious words. "Mission. Wellington." As if, by speaking them aloud, he could make all right again. "Mission."

Those perfumes were swirling around him once more. This time, they swept him off to a hot sunny hillside, where he found himself lying on springy grass, gazing up at the sky through yellow puffs of mimosa flowers, drinking in scents of lavender and rosemary. But with his next breath, the dark shrouds closed in again, suffocating him and swallowing the sky.

He wanted to cry out, to fight against the blanketing mists, but he did not have the strength. Their long grey fingers stroked him into darkness, deep as a pit.

Even in the darkness, there was pain. Piercing, unbearable pain, like daggers in his flesh. Ben tried to move, to throw them off, somehow, anyhow, but the enveloping web was looped around and under him, tying him in a tangled thicket from which it seemed he would never break free. And always the daggers. The daggers. He groaned and thrashed his body from side to side. If he was not dead, he must fight. *He must.*

"Sleep now," said a soft voice. It was barely a murmur but it soothed. It must have been sent from heaven. An angel? Cool clean linen was laid on his forehead, as refreshing as joyful rain on dry earth. Ben felt the knots unravel as his bonds receded into the grey mist, defeated by the angel's hand.

If I can sleep, I cannot be dead. If I can sleep... If I can only sleep...

It was not sleep that came. It was torture. Suddenly, he was being tossed back and forth between giants. And they were rejoicing at his groans of pain. This was not heaven. This was hell, full of red-hot needles and tongues of fire. From this, there could be no escape. His angel had forsaken him.

He cried out.

And his angel returned. His fair-haired angel. Calling his name, through the whirling flames. He wanted to reach for her, but he was pinioned. He could not escape.

"French," the angel said sternly. "You must speak only French. No English. Only French."

He was in a French heaven. Or was it hell? But his angel spoke French and so he must do so, too. "No English," he croaked.

Which language had he spoken? He could not tell. He could not hear his own voice. The circling shrouds were sucking it away, swallowing his words, swallowing everything. Were they trying to suck out his soul?

He gave a great cry of anguish. But it could not save him. The pit was opening at his feet and he was falling. Down, down, down.

Into blackness.

He must climb out of the pit. He must. If he could free his arms, he could climb. He could claw his way out of this blackness. He began to struggle against the invisible bonds that held him...

"Herr Benn."

It was his angel's voice. No, not hers. Another's. Another angel?

He struggled even harder to break free of the darkness. To reach her.

"Herr Benn, no. You will injure yourself. Wake up. Oh, pray, wake up."

A hand on his shoulder. Shaking him.

He was out of the pit. He could open his eyes. There was light. Bright, blinding light.

And his angel was still there, still there behind the light, still speaking to him in that sweet, urgent voice.

"Herr Benn. Oh, Herr Benn, you are yourself again. Thank heaven. You were having such a nightmare and I could not wake you. Are you...are you well now?"

She was speaking French to him. And the room was spinning. Had he really been dreaming? The pit was not real? Nor the giants with their red-hot needles?

A hand stroked a cooling cloth across his brow. Then it brought a cup to his lips and helped him to drink. The prickle of sharp lemon on his tongue was no dream. He was alive. This was real.

He turned his head a fraction to search for his angel's face, hoping desperately that she, too, was real.

Everything was blurred. The light was too bright. In desperation, he screwed up his eyes against it, struggling to focus. There was... Yes, he could make out a halo of fair curls filled with sunlight. And then, at last, a face.

He sighed out a long, thankful breath. His angel was still at his side. She was real.

And she was beautiful.

He did not know who she was, but all at once he understood the meaning of his dream. It was all true, even though it was a weird jumble of memories, interlaced with pain. He and Jack were on a spying mission for Wellington. They had been set upon by a gang of villains as they left Marseilles. And one of the assailants had had a gun.

"Did they shoot me?" he croaked, in French, gazing pleadingly at his angel. He was hot and aching. Covered in sweat. And the pain was certainly real. It seemed to be worst on his right side. He began to reach with his left hand, to find out how badly he was wounded.

Soft fingers caught his hand and held it. "Do not distress yourself, Herr Benn," the angel said, frowning down at him. "Yes, you were shot, but the bullet is gone and the wound is clean. Pray do not claw at your bandages. Your shoulder will heal better if you rest." She pushed him gently back on to feather pillows and laid his hand firmly on the coverlet.

"I… Where am I?" He had not seen this girl before, had he? She looked familiar and yet she was not. He would not have forgotten such fragile beauty.

She smiled at him. The frown melted away, leaving her skin smooth as a peach. "You are in Lyons. You were brought here by your friend, Mr Jacques, and my sister, Marguerite Grolier. You are safe here, in our weaving house."

That was why she seemed familiar. The silk-weaver was her sister. And he had seen the silk-weaver in his dreams, had he not? Had she not admonished him to speak only French?

He was having difficulty working out what was real and what was fantasy. "Jacques is here? I need to speak to him." Jack would be able to explain everything. Jack would set Ben's topsy-turvy memories to rights. Unless… "Jacques? Did they shoot him, too?"

"Be easy, sir. Your friend came off with a whole skin. As did my sister. You were the only casualty."

Ben sighed. What a relief. He said as much.

"For a German, you speak very good French, Herr Benn," she said, smiling broadly at him now. "You have very little accent."

Another piece of the puzzle slotted into place at her words. Ah yes. Since, unlike Jack, Ben could not speak French like a native, they had agreed that Ben would pretend to be a German. He had become Herr Christian Benn, while Jack had become Louis Jacques, a *bourgeois* from Paris. Ben must remember to play his part. Was there anything else that he needed to remember? And beware of?

He must speak French. Only French. No English.

And he must find out the name of this fair-haired angel.

She offered him the cup again and he drank greedily. "Thank you," he said. "Thank you, Miss...er... Your pardon, ma'am. I'm afraid I do not know your name."

"It is Grolier, of course. Suzanne Grolier."

"Suzanne." He repeated it several times, relishing the taste of the syllables on his tongue. "It is a beautiful name. It suits you."

She was blushing. "You must not say such things," she said, flustered. She grabbed the cup and made a great show of gathering up the linen she had been using to bathe his face. Then she retreated towards the door.

"Please don't go," Ben said.

"I must. You need to rest."

"But I cannot rest if I do not have your promise to return. Will you promise?"

Her blush was even deeper now, but after a moment she bit her lip and gave a tiny nod. "I will come back later to tend your wound. Provided you promise, in your turn, Herr Benn, to do everything I tell you to."

He frowned, puzzled. He was missing something important here.

She took a few steps forward so that she was standing at the end of the bed, looking gravely down at him. "You are an invalid. I am your nurse. A patient must obey his nurse or he will never get well." She smiled swiftly at him, a mischievous smile that lit up her delicate features. "You do want to get well, don't you, Herr Benn?"

If getting well would lose him that wonderful smile, he was not at all sure that he did.

• • • •

Safely back on the dark landing, Suzanne leant against the door and closed her eyes. Only for a second or two, while she tried to order her tumbling thoughts.

He was surely going to recover now. And he had said she was beautiful.

Did he feel it too, then? That extraordinary moment of recognition when she had first seen him, broken and bloody

6

on the floor of the old carriage, and known that they were meant for each other. One look was all it had taken. For her. Had he looked at Suzanne in the same way? Had he seen it, too?

Her practical self intervened. *He has only just regained his senses. He is badly wounded, and still very sick. He will need all his energies for staying alive.*

But he had said she was beautiful.

She sighed and shook her head to clear it. It didn't help. Her love, and her hopes, were fighting with her reason, and no amount of squabbling was going to produce a winner today. It was too soon. Herr Benn needed time to recover his health and strength. She would stay by his side while he did, and she would be able to see, soon enough, whether her love was returned. And in the meantime, she would remember how he had looked at her, his blue eyes very wide, and how he had repeated her name, caressing each syllable. Those were memories to treasure. Even if she could not be sure of exactly what they meant.

She smoothed her skirts and ran lightly down the stairs to find her sister in the kitchen, making coffee.

"What on earth have you been doing all this time?" Marguerite demanded. "We have to finish the Duchess of Courland's silk, and mama is having one of her bad days, and—"

Suzanne laid a consoling hand on her sister's arm to stop the stream of angry words. Marguerite, as the elder, carried most of the load of running their weaving house. If she was cross, she had cause. She had been doing all their chores while Suzanne sat stroking cooling cloths across her invalid's forehead. "I am sorry, Marguerite. I was with Herr Benn. He is awake at last and himself again. He spoke to me." She beamed at Marguerite. "You saved him and now he is going to get well."

"If he is awake, you should not be alone with him. It is most improper."

"What risk can he be to me when he is so ill?" Suzanne protested. "He needs a nurse, not a...a paramour. And there is no one else, is there? Berthe has to stay with mama and Guillaume has too much else to do, besides having hands that are far too rough for tending open wounds. You yourself said that we should not send Herr Benn to the nuns at the *Hôtel Dieu*."

"I think it was actually you who said that," Marguerite said with a gentle smile.

"Well, you were certainly the one who said we owed them a debt."

Marguerite took a long breath and sighed it out. "Yes, I did. And we do. Mr Jacques saved me when those men broke into my room in Marseilles. They would have taken all the silk." She shuddered. "I think they would have killed me, too."

"So, in return, we will nurse Mr Jacques's wounded companion until he is recovered," Suzanne said flatly. "*I* will nurse him."

"But—"

"You sound like Guillaume, Marguerite. He lectures me about the risk of losing my reputation. And—"

"And he is right."

Suzanne shook her head. "My reputation cannot be at risk unless someone in this house gossips about what I am doing. You would not, and neither would Berthe or Guillaume. So what is there to fear?" When Marguerite opened her mouth to protest again, Suzanne said placatingly, "I know you all have my best interests at heart. I have promised Guillaume that I will only dress his wound and take up his food. Guillaume is going to see to the rest, though I cannot imagine how he will find the time. And to allay your concerns, Marguerite, I will promise that...that I will not be alone with him once he is strong enough to rise from his bed. There. Will that content you?"

Marguerite shrugged. "I suppose it will have to." She shook her head and dropped a kiss on Suzanne's cheek.

Then she stiffened and said, "But remember, Suzanne, that we must be very careful. Mr Jacques and Herr Benn are strangers. We do not know where their sympathies lie. So we must say nothing—*nothing*—about ours. It is vital. You know it is. Promise me, Suzanne."

Suzanne could not understand why Marguerite was suddenly so wary of their guests. Did Marguerite know more that she was telling about Mr Jacques? They had spent several days on the road together, while Herr Benn was insensible, but still, it seemed to make little sense. "Surely these men would never betray us, no matter where their loyalties lie? You saved them."

"Men do strange things in the name of honour, Suzanne. And loyalty—loyalty to a cause—can be part of their code. Who knows what they might do, if their duty to their cause was in conflict with their gratitude to us? I would rather we did not test it."

"Pooh. In that case, I am surprised you allowed them into the house, given your poor opinion of them."

Marguerite shook her head sadly. "I sincerely hope that I am wrong to harbour doubts about them. But I do know that we are right to take care, with anyone and everyone. We both know that men need little excuse to fight. Royalists will attack Bonapartists who will attack royalists. If we appear to have no sympathies either way, no one will have grounds to molest us. You know how vulnerable we are here, Suzanne, with so many other houses ready to pounce on Grolier's. If they suspected the truth about papa, they would have swallowed us long since."

Fear gripped Suzanne. Herr Benn would never betray her, she was sure, but others might. And it would take only one ill-judged word. If the Groliers lost their independence, they would lose everything. And they had so many secrets to keep. She hung her head. "You are right, Marguerite. I am sorry. I promise."

Chapter Two

"BEN. *BEN.* FOR GOD'S SAKE, man, wake up."

The low, urgent whisper—and the fact that the voice was speaking English—penetrated Ben's uneasy doze. He managed to half-open one eye. Even that hurt. "Jack." His voice cracked on the single word. His throat was almost too dry for speech, but he had to know what was going on. "What on earth—?"

In reply, Jack clamped a brutal hand over Ben's mouth. The message could not have been clearer. *Silence.* Ben nodded his head a fraction, to tell his friend that he had understood, though in truth his mind was full of fog.

Jack removed his hand, but he was still frowning. "Listen," he hissed, in French. "We are in Lyons, in the house of Bonapartists. They are good people, but if they find out who we are, they are bound to have us arrested. So you must speak no English. Only French. Anything else will give us away. Do you understand, Ben? *Ben?* Do you understand what I'm saying to you?"

Ben understood pretty well, but Jack's grating whispers were hurting his head. He let it fall sideways on to the pillow and closed his eyes. For a second of respite. Then, recalling his duty, he opened them again and croaked, in French, "I could do with a drink."

Jack chuckled and gave him a mouthful of water.

Ben registered that his friend's frown had disappeared. Good. "Tell me what happened to me," Ben said, still in

French. "I was having such terrible nightmares. Daggers in my flesh, and black pits, and I seemed to be trapped in a fiendish thicket of twigs and brambles. I couldn't free myself."

"Poor old Ben." Jack glanced over his shoulder. The bedchamber door was safely shut. "Very well. But Miss Suzanne will only be gone for a few minutes. She is fetching hot water so I can clean you up a bit. We must not talk about anything important while she is here. We might let something slip." He waited for Ben's nod of agreement before continuing. "You collapsed after you were shot. Miss Grolier—Marguerite Grolier, that is, the silk-weaver I rescued from those ruffians at the inn—helped us to escape in her coach. She was very brave. She faced down five armed men, all by herself. It was astonishing. Especially from a *bourgeoise*." He shook his head, gazing vaguely into the middle distance, as if at an image that only he could see.

Ben muttered impatiently. He didn't want to hear about Miss Marguerite. He wanted to know about himself. And about the beautiful Suzanne.

"We hid you on the floor of the coach, under the parcels of silk. We had to tie you down so that you wouldn't roll about. And—I'm sorry, but it was necessary—Marguerite dosed you with laudanum." Jack shrugged. It was almost an apology. "We had to keep you quiet."

"I suppose so," Ben admitted. Tied down and sedated with laudanum? No wonder he'd had such appalling dreams. The stuff had always disagreed with him.

"I'm afraid that we weren't able to get the ball out of your shoulder until we reached Rognac. It was too risky to stop earlier. And the surgeon I found there was a bit of a butcher. You'll have a nasty scar." Jack was now looking a bit guilty.

A butcher of a surgeon. That accounted for the daggers in his flesh, too. Ben sighed. "You only did what you had to do. What matters is the mission, remember?"

11

"Yes. And it's more urgent than ever. Bonaparte has escaped from Elba. He's back in France. No doubt he's planning to reclaim his throne."

"But King Louis—"

"Louis is not loved. Bonaparte is. And he is clever. There's no knowing what he'll be able to do. So I'm going to ride south today and see what I can discover about his movements. That means leaving you alone here, though. In a Bonapartist house. Can you cope with that?"

"Yes," Ben said stoutly. "As long as no one gives me any more laudanum." He managed a grin, which Jack returned. "Are you really sure the Groliers are Bonapartists? How do you know?"

Jack nodded. "You didn't hear how enthusiastically Marguerite cried '*Vive l'Empereur!*' when we learned of the little tyrant's escape from exile. If you had, you'd be in no doubt. I had to pretend that I'm a Bonapartist, too, or I might have been rumbled. I fancy most of Lyons supports the man. If he ever gets this far north..." Jack shrugged again and sighed. They both knew the risks. If Napoleon Bonaparte raised an army, Europe could go up in flames, all over again.

At that moment, Ben heard footsteps outside the door. Jack heard them too, and put a finger to his lips. Ben nodded and lay back on his pillows. He needed to think about all this, to work out what he must do, but he was so very tired. And he ached, everywhere. At the sound of the door opening, he gave up the struggle and allowed himself to drift off into sleep.

• • • •

In the days following his whispered exchange with Jack, Ben did little but worry, during almost every waking hour. He worried about Jack, riding off on his own through enemy territory, hoping to glean intelligence about the tyrant's progress. He worried that if Jack said a word out of place, he could be arrested and shot. And should he not have returned by now, in any case?

12

Ben worried about his own position, too. He was so damnably weak. He still could barely move. He certainly could not travel—Suzanne was insisting on that—and so he was useless as a spy, besides being a burden to Jack. If Jack made it back to Lyons safely, Ben would insist that he carry on alone, for the information they had was vital. Their mission mattered above everything. Jack had to carry the intelligence to London. And if that meant leaving Ben alone in Lyons, surrounded by the enemy, so be it.

No matter how much Ben tried, he was not able to convince himself that Suzanne was a Bonapartist. She had given no sign of any interest in politics, in all the hours she had spent tending his wound.

Ben now knew quite a lot about this little household but nothing at all about where its loyalties lay. The mother was an invalid, and somewhat unstable, following a terrible carriage accident some years before. Privately, Ben suspected that Madame Grolier had been sent stark mad by the blow to her head, though no one ever used such words to describe her. The father was abroad, Suzanne said, travelling to find buyers for Grolier silk and velvet. Suzanne had shown Ben samples of the beautiful, and costly, products of their looms. The fabrics were finer than anything to be had in London, he was sure.

In the father's absence, Marguerite was in charge of the weaving house. The two sisters did most of the weaving work, too, for there were only two elderly household servants plus a simpleton kitchen boy. Ben suspected that the family was living hand to mouth. Not surprising, on reflection, given the fact that France had been at war for so many years. Who would have the money to buy precious silk in a country where the price of food was so high?

Whatever their politics, the Groliers were good, generous people and Ben wished he could help them. He owed them his life, that was certain. Perhaps, if King Louis's forces defeated the upstart, things would quieten down? Perhaps Ben would be able to tell Suzanne the truth about himself? He hated deceiving her. She deserved better of him in return for all the dedicated care she had given him.

It was astonishing how quickly they had fallen into the way of being easy with one another. Several times a day, Suzanne would come to Ben's cramped little chamber on the first-floor landing to check the dressing on his wound. She always seemed to find an excuse to linger and to talk. And he was in no hurry to persuade her to leave.

She was a gentle, kind and beautiful girl. And she had the speech and manners of a lady. If he had not known the truth of it, he would never have dreamed she was only a *bourgeoise*.

• • • •

The bedchamber door opened very quietly. Ben's head jerked up. He had not heard a knock.

"Oh!" Suzanne cried, springing up from the bed where she was sitting. Her hand had been so close to Ben's. Almost touching, but not quite. In another few minutes, he might have been holding her hand, for the very first time.

"Good evening, ma'am," Jack said from the doorway, bowing. "I trust I see you well? I clearly have no need to enquire after my friend here. I can see that, under your tender care, he has improved beyond measure while I have been away."

Suzanne, now scarlet in the face, dipped him a tiny curtsey and fled past him.

"Oh, dear," Jack said, looking anything but remorseful, "I seem to have frightened her away."

Jack had always loved to play the wicked rogue with women. It was not fair on Suzanne, but Ben knew it would be unwise to scold him. That would only make him even more suspicious of what Ben and Suzanne might have been doing. So Ben grinned back and said, "Looking like that, you would frighten anyone." It was true. Jack was filthy. And he smelt. "What on earth have you done to yourself, Jack?"

14

Jack tapped a finger against his nose and went to close the door securely. Then he came back to take Suzanne's place on the bed. "You would be equally disreputable if you'd ridden as many miles as I have, these last few days. But I can tell you, I watched the most astonishing sight of my life. Had I not seen it with my own eyes, I would not have believed it."

That was too much for Ben. "Tell me," he urged. "Tell me all of it."

Jack described how he had ridden south and found royalist soldiers massed in every town and a whole regiment in Grenoble. Finally, hiding behind rocks in a narrow pass on the Gap road, he had seen a regiment of the King's soldiers blockading the road, muskets at the ready. Facing them, just out of range, was the Imperial Guard. "Their formation was immaculate. They had been struggling over mountain passes for days, but no one would have known. They looked formidable. And even I could tell they were spoiling for a fight."

"And Bonaparte? You saw him?"

Jack nodded. "I missed him at first. I'd expected more splendour. His horse was nothing remarkable and his dress certainly wasn't—a plain grey coat and a broad black hat, like a merchant's. He sat his horse in front of the Guard while the two sides stared each other out. The silence was uncanny. He was scrutinising the ranks of royalist troops as though he were reviewing them on the parade square. When he'd done with that, he walked his horse forward, cool as you like, until he was well within musket range. No one made a move to shoot. Then he dismounted, quite casually, and walked towards the guns. One small vulnerable figure facing certain death. Such supreme confidence. Such courage." Jack swallowed audibly.

Ben held his breath.

"He looked at each man in the front rank and addressed the regiment as if he recognised them. When all their eyes were on him, he even smiled. And then he put his bare hand over his heart and challenged them. 'Soldiers of the Fifth! If there is any man among you who would shoot his General—his Emperor—let him do it!' By God, it was magnificent." Jack's eyes were shining.

"I take it they didn't shoot?" Ben put in acidly.

Jack gave a snort of laughter. "No. There was a long silence, as if everyone was holding their breath, and suddenly the whole of the Fifth was yelling '*Vive l'Empereur!*' and surrounding him. I tell you, Ben, the Emperor Napoleon has truly come into his own again." He paused and shook his head. "He may be only a puffed-up little Corsican, but I cannot fault his courage. Or his understanding of men. They love him, and everything he stands for. I'm sure they are all ready to die for him."

Ben sighed. "It's a very potent mixture. Wellington is admired and respected, but he is not loved. We have no one who inspires such devotion."

"I fear you're right," Jack agreed. "The man's recreating his old legend. I'd wager the troops in Grenoble will fall under his spell the moment he gets there. Probably Lyons as well."

Ben closed his eyes and let out a long breath. This was really important information. If only he were not so weak and helpless…

Jack was starting to look anxious. "I know you're not really fit to travel yet, Ben," he began tentatively, "but we've got to get this news back to England. They'll have to muster the Allied armies again. And quickly, too, or else—"

Ben was having none of it. With a huge effort, he pushed himself up off the pillows. "I'm not fit to go, Jack. We both know that. You must go on alone." He seized Jack's arm. "The mission comes first."

"No. We'll manage. We can—"

"Stubble it, Jack. You know we can't. You're the leader. You have to leave me." Exhausted, he fell back.

Jack grimaced. "You're right," he admitted, at last. "I'll have to go alone. Tomorrow. But I'll see you before I leave and get you to somewhere safer. If you stay here among the enemy, you'll probably end up being shot."

Ben smiled and shook his head. "You know, Jack, I honestly think that the Grolier household is the safest place in the world for me at present."

"What?" Jack frowned for a moment. Then, "Oh, so that's the way of it? Well, I wish you joy of her. But make sure you don't end up in parson's mousetrap with a French *bourgeoise* you daren't present to your grandfather." He rose and made for the door. "And make sure you get home in one piece. too. The Honours need you. If you don't appear, I'll be back to fetch you, pretty French mistress or no."

By the time Ben had gathered enough wits to swear at his friend, Jack had gone.

Chapter Three

SUZANNE FELT AS IF HER whole body was glowing. She glanced across at Herr Benn. They had become so comfortable together and, now that he was definitely on the mend, she did not need to worry quite so much about his recovery. She allowed herself to relax, to savour this precious time with him. Eventually, she would have to stop being alone with him—had she not promised Marguerite that these visits would cease once Herr Benn was well enough to get out of bed?—but he could not compromise her as he was. He was still much too weak to rise.

She refused to think about what would happen once he was well enough to leave, for she could not bear to think about losing him. She had to keep living in the moment. With him. Seeing him. Touching him. She gazed round the tiny box room where he was kept hidden. It seemed bigger and brighter than usual. The colours were more vivid and the scent of her lavender water was surprisingly tangy. Was that what love did to the senses?

Benn flapped his good arm and groaned.

Suzanne turned back to him in concern. "Are you in pain?"

"No." He grinned up at her from his pillows. "But I'm bored, lying here trussed up like a parcel. I'd so like to be up and about. To find out what is going on."

She immediately responded in the same light-hearted tone. "Oh, I can tell you that, sir. It seems we missed a great spectacle. You've heard of the Comte d'Artois, the King's brother? Well, he ordered the regiment here in Lyons to muster at first light this morning. He wanted to hold a formal review." She chuckled. "Apparently, it was a shambles. Instead of saluting him, half the regiment made faces at him. He's a ridiculous little man, and he deserves to be laughed at, but—"

"The troops rebelled?"

"They started shouting for their emperor. The moment the count saw it was all up with him, he turned tail and rode off for Paris." When Herr Benn began struggling to sit up, she protested, "Please, Herr Benn, you must not exert yourself." She put a hand on his good shoulder and tried to push him back onto his pillows.

He shook her off, though it clearly caused him pain. "Bonaparte," he gasped. "Is he here in Lyons?"

That was when Suzanne remembered her other promise to her sister. Every word was dangerous, Marguerite said, even to a German like Herr Benn. And Suzanne had failed her.

"Tell me." Herr Benn was almost shouting. "Is Bonaparte here?"

"I…" She couldn't move. His fierce stare was pinning her in place. "Yes," she admitted at last, in a tiny voice. "He is here. And the army has gone over to him."

Herr Benn's face changed in an instant. She had never seen such bleak determination. "Jacques. I have to go," he muttered, using his good arm to throw back the bedclothes.

"No." Suzanne tried desperately to hold him down, but he pushed her off. In his agitation, his strength seemed to have increased tenfold.

"I have to go," he said again. He swung his bare feet to the floor and pulled himself up. For a moment, he stood there, swaying. Then he muttered something Suzanne could not catch and forced his way past her, even as she leapt up to stop him.

He rounded the corner of the bed, making for the door. For a moment, he stood straight and strong, but then he stumbled and fell forward.

His head hit the corner of the chest. Suzanne heard a crack like a pistol shot. "Benn!" she screamed, throwing herself towards him. She was too late. His head was already covered in blood. And he had passed out. He might even be dead. She screamed again, in panic. "Marguerite! Guillaume! Come quickly!"

Suzanne was still kneeling helplessly by Benn's inert body when Marguerite and Guillaume arrived. Marguerite took one look and sent Guillaume back downstairs for hot water and fresh bandages.

"Don't look so concerned, my love," Marguerite said calmly, dropping to her knees to check Benn's pulse. "He's alive. And head wounds always bleed like this." She used her handkerchief to mop the blood away so that she could examine the wound more closely. "It's not all that deep. Herr Benn probably has a very hard head. I'm sure he'll soon mend."

How could Marguerite make jokes at a time like this? Could she not see that Herr Benn was in great danger? His shoulder wound had opened again. His bandages were getting redder and redder. He might die at any moment. Suzanne clasped her hands even more tightly together and prayed desperately.

Her prayers were answered. Guillaume returned unbelievably quickly.

"Put the water down by the bed," Marguerite said coolly. "Then help me to lift him. Once we have dressed his hurts, we must not move him again."

Suzanne watched, helpless and shivering with shock, as her sister and Guillaume lifted Herr Benn on to the bed.

Marguerite tended the head wound first. She bathed it gently and bound it up with a linen pad. The bandage covered his left eye, though it had taken no hurt. "He will have to manage with one eye for a while," she said lightly.

"Head wounds are very difficult to bandage." She smiled over her shoulder at Suzanne.

Suzanne could not smile back. Nor could she move. She stayed where she was on the floor, praying.

Marguerite shrugged and instructed Guillaume to help her remove Herr Benn's blood-soaked bandages. Working swiftly and carefully, she cleaned the shoulder wound and applied a new, larger pad to absorb the fresh bleeding. "Now we must make him comfortable and keep him warm," she said, tying the last bandage. She rinsed her hands and rose to her feet. "Suzanne, I shall need that blanket you have there."

It was only then that Suzanne realised there was a blanket round her shoulders. Who had put it there? And when? Marguerite presumably, when Suzanne had started to shiver.

"*Suzanne*. Herr Benn is becoming chilled."

He was not chilled. He was ashen. Surely he must be dead? Suzanne's eyes filled with tears. "He is dead!" she cried in anguish.

Marguerite took Suzanne's arm and forced her to her feet. "He is not dead," she said in a rallying voice. "See for yourself." She checked his pulse again and said, "His heart is beating strongly. He will recover soon enough."

It was too much. Suzanne threw herself on her knees by the bed, seized Herr Benn's hand in hers and kissed the warm, living flesh. Yes, he was alive. Her tears were flowing strongly now, but they were tears of relief. Her love was alive. He would recover. And it would be her task to nurse him back to health.

She took a deep breath and scrubbed away her tears with the back of her hand. There was work to do.

"How came he to be out of bed?" Marguerite asked quietly.

Guilt seized Suzanne. "It was my fault," she admitted, digging out a handkerchief to blow her nose. "I was telling him about that ridiculous scene with the Comte d'Artois.

21

Oh, don't frown at me, Marguerite. I know now that I did wrong. But I never thought I was doing any harm. Herr Benn is a German, after all. What does he care whether France is ruled by a king or an emperor? But he did seem to care. He insisted on knowing if Bonaparte had arrived. He became agitated. I could not keep him in bed. He tried to walk but he was not strong enough for more than a few steps. He fell and hit his head on the corner of that chest. It was all my fault. I...I am sorry."

Marguerite patted her shoulder. "It was an unfortunate accident. I doubt there was anything you could have done to prevent it. And now you must rest. You have had a severe shock."

No. She had to stay here, to tend to her invalid. She protested strongly.

Marguerite was insistent. She forced Suzanne to return to her own room and lie down on her bed. "Guillaume and I will look after Herr Benn. I promise." She smiled as she tucked a blanket tenderly round Suzanne. A moment later, the bedchamber door clicked shut behind her.

Suzanne gazed up into nothingness. She was shivering again. How could she be so cold at this time of year?

She tried to bring some order to her thoughts. Eventually she succeeded, after a struggle. She accepted that she was in no fit state to nurse Herr Benn at the moment. She knew Marguerite could be trusted to do whatever was required. For now. But later—tomorrow, perhaps even tonight—Suzanne would return to her invalid's bedside. He needed loving hands to tend to his hurts. They would be Suzanne's hands.

With her mind now at rest, she snuggled into the warm blankets. She would allow herself to sleep. Just for an hour.

Chapter Four

"WEREN'T YOU SUPPOSED TO leave for Paris yesterday?" Ben asked anxiously, the moment Jack appeared in his room.

"Er...yes, but I was...er...unavoidably delayed."

There was something smoky going on here. Jack was looking guilty and avoiding Ben's eye. "Delayed?" Ben repeated. "What do you mean? How *delayed*?"

Jack coloured. Then the words came out in a rush. "If you must know, I spent most of yesterday tied to a chair in the attic."

"What?"

Jack laughed self-consciously. "It's a long story. And I'm ashamed to have to admit that I was outwitted by a woman. By Marguerite, in fact. From something she overheard, she...er...she thought I was leaving in order to betray you to Bonaparte, so she...er...drugged my coffee and locked me up. She was going to keep me there until you were well enough to leave Lyons, I think. You're a lucky man, you know, Ben. She was trying to save your neck."

Ben's jaw dropped. "But she's a Bonapartist. You said so. Why on earth would she do such a thing?"

Jack shook his head. "No, I was wrong about the Groliers. Dead wrong. This is a royalist household. Marguerite and I have discovered we're on the same side.

And she's going to help us." He was jubilant now. And too loud in Ben's ear.

Ben groaned. All this was more than his poor head could take in. "I've got the devil of a headache, Jacques. Do we really have to keep speaking French? It would be so much easier on my addled wits if—"

"You must stick to French," Jack insisted. "Your…er…native tongue might be easier on your cracked pate, but it could be dangerous." He dropped his voice to a low murmur, so soft that Ben could barely make out the words. "It's safest if they keep believing you're German and I'm French. And walls have ears, you know."

Suzanne was not the enemy. It was wonderful to have it confirmed, though Ben had always felt it must be so. She was an ally, and a friend. But it was clear from Jack's warning that she still did not know Ben was English. And Jack was surely right. It was safest to keep it that way. Safest for Suzanne. He mumbled agreement.

"What happened to your head? They told me it was an accident. Is that true?"

"My own stupid clumsiness again. You didn't come to say farewell yesterday as you'd promised, and then Suzanne told me that Bonaparte had arrived in Lyons, so I assumed something must have happened to you. Must say I'm not totally sure what I intended to do once I got out of this room, but…" Ben tried to shrug, but it hurt too much. He gave up the attempt.

"Thank you for your concern. Still, I am here now. And I will complete the mission alone, as we agreed. But I have yet to find a way."

Ben's body was not working well, but at least his brain seemed to be functioning again. He laughed softly at the audacity of his idea. "Why not enlist with Bonaparte? You could pass for one of his supporters. You always were a plausible rogue. The army is bound to accompany their precious emperor to Paris, so you would have plenty of chances to gather information. And once you'd reached

Paris, you could melt away. It's a good plan, don't you think?"

"Another one of your hare-brained schemes. Still, it might work if—"

Before Jack could finish, the door was flung open and Marguerite marched into the room. Hands on hips, she glowered at them. "It is a ridiculous plan. Have you no idea how the army operates? Soldiers who 'melt away', as you call it, are shot for desertion."

Ben was so shocked he could not say a word. But Jack seemed to take it all in his stride. He rose lazily to his feet and bowed to her. He was actually laughing.

Embarrassed, Ben gulped and tried to speak.

Jack silenced him with a raised hand. "It seems I was right to say that walls have ears, Benn," he said, though his eyes were riveted on Marguerite's face.

"No, sir," she retorted. "Not walls. Doors."

Jack laughed as if he were enjoying himself. But Marguerite was beginning to look very anxious. She set about trying to persuade Jack that it would be suicide for him to travel alone to Paris. Jack, in typical fashion, airily dismissed all her arguments. "I must do my duty," he finished flatly. When she bristled, he added, "But I will take no unnecessary risks, I promise you."

She was clearly not mollified. "If you are determined to go to Paris, Jacques, I shall go with you," she said.

"No. You cannot. You—"

She silenced him with a finger across his lips.

Ah. So that was how the land lay. Ben was tempted to berate his friend—wasn't it Jack who had sternly warned Ben against falling in love with a *bourgeoise*? But then he saw how the pair were gazing at each other, and thought better of it.

"We shall travel together, as silk merchants whose only interest is in selling our wares," Marguerite announced calmly. "We shall be carrying the Duchess of Courland's silk. We merchants make no distinction between royalists

25

and Bonapartists, provided their coin is good. There will be no difficulty, I assure you. I have done this before."

"Too dangerous," Jack snapped. "Out of the question. I forbid it."

Ben decided it was time for him to intervene, for Jack seemed to be forgetting that their mission came first. "I think you should listen to her, Jacques," he began in the most reasonable voice he could muster. "Oh, don't turn your temper on me. I'm an invalid. And immune. If Miss Marguerite is prepared to help us, for the cause that we all believe in, we must consider, coolly and rationally, whether her plan is more likely to succeed than yours." He grinned at Jack's impotent fury. "I tell you candidly, my friend, that I think she is right. You should travel to Paris together."

• • • •

Suzanne was once again in Herr Benn's bedchamber when her sister came looking for her to have a private word. Marguerite insisted they went downstairs to sit by the fire. Intrigued, Suzanne agreed, though she was loath to leave her invalid.

"I am leaving tomorrow for Paris," Marguerite explained. "We shall take a trunk of samples and the Duchess of Courland's silk."

"We...?" Suzanne asked, puzzled. "You travel with Guillaume?"

"I am travelling with Jacques. I... Oh, Suzanne, he is not a Bonapartist after all. He is a royalist. And a spy for the English."

Suzanne gasped. Was it possible? But if Marguerite was sure, it must be so.

"While I am gone, you must take charge of the household. And of Herr Benn..."

Suzanne smiled and nodded. She was more than happy to do both.

"...who is also a spy," Marguerite went on evenly. "And an Englishman, besides."

Suzanne was so shocked she could not say a word. Not a German? English? An English spy?

"I'm afraid I deceived you," Marguerite said, colouring a little. "I discovered that Herr Benn was English on the journey from Marseilles—when he was delirious, he spoke English, though no one else heard him and he probably doesn't even remember doing it. I told no one, not even you, because I thought it was the best way to protect him. I…I thought Jacques was a Bonapartist who would betray him. I am so glad I was wrong."

Suzanne let out a long breath and struggled to get her thoughts in order. Yes, it did make a kind of sense. And it meant that taking care of Benn—hiding him—was even more important than she had imagined. She would do it. And take pride in it.

Marguerite, having finished her confession, had quickly changed to a safer subject, the handling of the weaving business and the many things that Suzanne would have to do. "There are unlikely to be many customers while the times are so uncertain," she finished.

Suzanne drew herself up. "I have taken charge before. I can do so again."

"But that was for a few days only," Marguerite objected. "This time I might be gone for…" She broke off, swallowing. Then she gave a little nod. "I am sure you will cope extremely well."

"Thank you," Suzanne said. She knew that it was true. Loving Herr Benn had changed her, made her more capable, more confident. She smiled at Marguerite.

"I suggest you move Herr Benn into my chamber once I am gone," Marguerite said. "It is much bigger than that cramped box room and will make it easier for Guillaume to see to his needs. You know that you must stop nursing him, do you not? It is most improper for an unmarried girl to do so, especially without a chaperon."

"No!" Suzanne protested hotly. "He needs gentle care. I am the only one able to dress his wounds properly while he is so weak." She raised her chin. "I love him, Marguerite, and I am sure he loves me in return. I know I am in no danger from him. He would never harm me. We love each other. And that is all that matters."

Marguerite—who was usually so ready with arguments on every topic—blushed rosily and, to Suzanne's surprise, began to talk of the practical arrangements for her departure on the morrow.

Chapter Five

BEN CLOSED HIS UNBANDAGED eye and relaxed into the feather pillows to enjoy the sensation of Suzanne's hands on his body. As always, she was precise and careful in removing the dressings from his wounds. With his eyes shut, the touch of her fingers on his naked torso was utterly delightful, as if she had laid one of her sumptuous silken velvets on his chest and swept it slowly across his skin. He floated, half awake, half dreaming.

"Mmm." The sigh of pleasure escaped before he was aware of it. His body might be weak as water, but every square inch of it trembled at the mere prospect of Suzanne's touch. He sank deeper into the pillows. His bones were melting.

"Ouch." The dressing had caught. A stab of pain shattered the fragile fantasy that had been cradling him.

"Oh, forgive me, Herr Benn," Suzanne gasped. Her fingers stilled for a moment, but it was too late. His shoulder wound had begun to bleed again. She caught up a fresh dressing and tried to wipe away the blood, working carefully and gently, as she always did.

With her sister gone, she was now in sole charge of the weaving house, but she was still finding time to nurse him, just as before. And even though she had learned that he was an English spy, she had never asked to know his real name. She seemed content to keep using his *nom de guerre*. On reflection, it was probably for the best. If she were to discover that he was actually an English aristocrat, their comfortable understanding might cease. That would hurt unbearably.

Without thinking, Ben slid his good hand over hers and held it. She started, but she did not try to pull away. He absorbed the heat of her body through his fingers, as if he were basking in her sun. It was perfect. He had wanted to do this for so long.

Was that a tiny shiver?

She had frozen in her place. She was refusing to look at him.

In the blink of an eye, Ben's sun-filled warmth evaporated. His fingers felt as if they had been doused with icy water, as if his flesh were shrinking away from hers, even though neither of them had moved.

He bit down on a curse. What on earth was he about? He was behaving towards this amazingly courageous girl as if she were some kind of loose woman. She was his nurse and his rescuer. She deserved better than to be turned into an object of his lust.

He lifted his hand away. "Your pardon, Suzanne," he began in a low voice. "I did not intend to alarm you."

Her glance flickered to his face and away again. Her cheek was flushed. The delicate rose pink became her much too well, reminding him yet again of why his body's desires were threatening to overcome his sense of honour.

It must not happen. They had become close by force of circumstances as she dressed and redressed his wounds. No matter what he felt for Suzanne—and he was ashamed to admit it was lust—he must not allow her to feel anything for him.

She was a gentle, shy and hardworking girl, with little experience of men. She might too easily come to feel more for Ben than she should. And then what would happen? As soon as he was well enough, he would have to abandon her to continue with his mission. It was his duty to do so. He must make sure she was able to forget him. That was his duty, too.

It was different back home in England. The girls he met there were of his own class. If they chose to flirt, or to swoon over his cursed good looks and the viscount's title he would one day inherit, that was their choice. They knew the rules of the game.

But Suzanne did not know those rules. She was no aristocrat, merely a French silk-weaver's daughter. The game she played was a game of life and death, for she was a supporter of King Louis in a country that was wildly cheering the return of its beloved Emperor Napoleon from exile. Worse, she was hiding and nursing an English spy. She must not be allowed to develop tender feelings for such a dangerous guest.

Soon they would part for good, and Ben must leave her with a whole heart. His honour demanded nothing less.

• • • •

Suzanne's hand felt as if it were burning. It was the first time Benn had willingly touched her. And it was something as simple as laying his fingers over hers. Was it a lover's caress? Suzanne could not be sure, but she felt as if her whole being was aglow. All at once, her throat was so tight and dry that she wondered if she would ever be able to speak again. The man she loved was caressing her fingers. The glory of it shivered through her.

And in that same moment he broke the contact with a murmured apology. As if it had been a mistake. *No.*

The word screamed in her head, but she was unable to make a sound. She could not move, either. She risked a glance at his face. Before, his expression had been open and even gentle, but now there was a shadow of concern. He was troubled. And something more. He wore a puzzled frown, as if he had been presented with a conundrum he could not solve.

Was that how he viewed her? As a puzzle?

31

He swallowed a sound that could have been a groan. He was in pain. His shoulder was bleeding. Suzanne pushed her doubts to the back of her mind. What mattered now was her role as Benn's nurse.

Deftly, she eased the rest of the dressing from his shoulder wound. The fresh bleeding had loosened it. She bit her lip as she worked, for it had been her fault. She had been so full of the joy of his touch that she had not paid enough attention to the mundane business of removing his bandages. And so she had hurt him and possibly set back his recovery.

A little voice whispered that she should be glad, for as soon as he was recovered, he would leave. He was a spy, after all, with a mission to fulfil. In her heart, she knew she was betraying her family's royalist cause by wishing to keep him hidden here and under her own care. For a moment, she felt truly guilty, but then her logical mind began to fight back. There was no real urgency. Benn's French companion had already left for Paris with Marguerite. The intelligence they carried would presumably be sent to England with all speed, via their embassy in the capital.

What purpose would it serve for Benn to rise from his sickbed to follow them? Nothing of note had happened since they left. Bonaparte was still here in Lyons, basking in the adulation of the crowds, and issuing imperial proclamations, right and left. No doubt he would leave for Paris soon, but Marguerite and Jacques were days ahead of him. They would be safe.

Suzanne eased Benn up from the pillows to pass the bandage behind his back. The tips of her fingers slid across smooth skin and leashed muscle. Even with his head half-swathed in bandages, Benn was beautiful to look at, with his thick blond hair and his finely sculpted features, but his body was all male—lithe, powerful and hard.

She shivered again.

"Tickling an invalid is unfair, you know." He was grinning up at her. The fine skin at the corner of his unbandaged eye was crinkled with good humour. Was he deliberately teasing her? Could he feel her tension?

She attempted to respond in kind. "An invalid must be kept in his place, sir. Which is under the thumb of his nurse."

Oh dear. Had she gone too far? She quickly secured the bandage round his torso. The bleeding had stopped, thank goodness. "And now for your head," she said, briskly efficient. She unwound the bandage with care, but she need not have worried. His head was mending much more quickly than his shoulder. His head wound had bled a great deal, but the cut was not deep.

"I imagine it should be possible to leave off this bandage now," she said. "Your scalp will heal more quickly if it is open to the air."

"I should certainly prefer to have the use of both my eyes. With two eyes, I am better able to appreciate the view." He grinned at his own wit.

Quite incorrigible. Suzanne ignored his grin and concentrated on his wound. "It was your own fault for trying to leave your bed." She was trying, not very successfully, to sound stern. "And head wounds are extremely difficult to bandage. If we hadn't taken it across your eye, it would have slipped off. All that hair of yours gets in the way, you know. Perhaps I should shave it off?"

"Spare me, lady."

Their normal, comfortable rapport was back. It was a huge relief. Suzanne smiled primly down at him. "Your trouble, Benn, is that you set far too much store by your looks. It would teach you a well-earned lesson if I did shave your head. Some of it *will* have to be cut," she added, more seriously. "I dare not wash out the matted blood, for your wound must be kept dry."

"You will do only what is necessary, I know. Teasing aside, Suzanne, I do trust you. Without your care, I could well be dead." He raised his good hand as if to touch her again. It hung suspended for a moment. Then he let it fall back on to his chest. He smiled, but it looked forced. "Do as you will with me, ma'am. I am far too feeble to resist you."

With an effort, Suzanne shook her head at him. They would be together for some weeks more, while he recovered. And resistance was a quality she had still to learn.

Chapter Six

THE DAYS AND WEEKS OF CARING for Benn were taking their toll on Suzanne. Every visit to his chamber was more difficult that the last. Today, she had managed to retain her composure until she reached her own bedchamber, but it was a close-run thing. She locked her door and almost collapsed against it.

What on earth was happening to her? Oh, she loved Herr Benn. She had known that from the first time she set eyes on him. But did love have to bring such weakness of mind and body?

She had simply taken him coffee. It was part of their early morning ritual, but it had never been anything other than very proper. This morning, her fingers had brushed against his when she retrieved his cup. It had not been intentional on her side. And on his? He had deliberately held her hand once before, but she knew he regretted it, for the gesture had never been repeated. She had been so naïve at first, so sure that he returned her love. However, all these weeks of nursing him had proved her wrong. He was polite, friendly and extremely grateful to her, but he had done nothing more to suggest that he might one day come to love her.

One day? What was she thinking of? Thanks to her care, he would soon be healed. Soon—much too soon—he would be gone, travelling alone through enemy France, ready to risk his life for his country and his cause. It was her cause, too, but she was increasingly torn between her devotion to King Louis and her longing to keep Benn by her side. If she had to choose, where would her loyalties lie?

Suzanne clutched her hands together and began to walk back and forth across the threadbare rug, forcing her wobbly limbs to move. She was not a weakling. She was a grown woman. She was capable of taking charge of her family's entire weaving business. So why could she not take charge of her own emotions, her own heart?

Because it is given. It is no longer yours to control.

She gulped, shook her head against that traitorous thought, and dug her fingernails into her palms, in hopes that pain might force her back to reality.

It did not. The pain was real enough, but the siren voice in the back of her mind refused to be silenced.

You have very little time left to discover the truth of what he feels for you. Once he leaves Lyons, leaves you, he will not return, unless you prove to him that he has no choice. Now is not the time for missish airs and ladylike flirtations. You can no longer claim the title of "lady", in any case. If you want him to love you, as you love him, you have only days to make it so.

Suzanne could have sworn that her inner voice laughed. It was a low, sensuous sound. And it was followed by soft, seductive words, stealing into her mind and settling like a contented cat.

If you would win all, Suzanne, you must dare to risk all.

She stopped dead and clapped her hands to her ears, trying to shut out the sound. It was useless. The words, the thought, the subtle laughter, all were imprisoned inside her and echoing around the walls of her mind. Such a thought, once confronted, could not be banished, no matter how wicked it might be. Was she really, truly, thinking of giving herself to a man she barely knew? Was she ready to forfeit her honour, solely in order to tempt an English spy to love her?

She sank down on to her bed and covered her eyes. She was mad. She must be. It was wrong, wicked, foolish. She sighed deeply. It was all of those things, and yet she still wanted him. For she loved him, beyond reason, even if he could not love her in return.

Heaven help her. She was lost.

• • • •

Ben frowned, considering. This morning, something was very wrong with Suzanne. She was far from her usual positive self. What could be worrying her? There was a multitude of possibilities. It might be the weaving business, which she had been left to run all on her own since her sister's departure; it might be the antics of the so-called Emperor Napoleon on his triumphal progress towards Paris; or it might be something else altogether. What worried Ben was the fact that Suzanne was refusing to share her concerns with him. When she returned, he would ask her outright.

Ben shifted on his pillows and winced when pain lanced through his shoulder. His confounded wound was taking far too long to heal. He should have been back on his feet by now and on his way home to England.

That thought gave him pause. There had been no news from Jack and Marguerite. Bonaparte himself must surely be in Paris by now. That could mean real danger for Jack. Oh, if only this cursed wound would heal. If only—

The door opened. Ben looked up eagerly, smiling automatically at the prospect of seeing Suzanne again, even though it was less than half an hour since she had left him. Her presence had come to mean more to him that he dared to admit, even to himself.

But this time it was not Suzanne. It was Guillaume, the old manservant. He was carrying a jug of steaming water and, as usual, his face was inscrutable.

He began to lay out Ben's shaving tackle. "Shall I do it for you, sir?"

Ben shook his head. "Thank you, Guillaume, but as I am left-handed, I am able to manage it pretty well myself now. Perhaps you would hold the mirror?"

Guillaume nodded.

Ben began to lather his face. He found he was perversely glad that Suzanne was not here, offering such intimate services. No doubt the household assumed the worst about their mistress spending time alone with Ben. There was always gossip, even in a tiny household such as this one.

Ben was doing Suzanne an injustice, he decided firmly. She might be only a *bourgeoise* but she would not allow her servants to comment on her conduct. Only her mother had the right to do that, but Madame Grolier seemed to live in a fantasy world of her own making. She probably did not even know Ben was in the house.

"A little higher," Ben said, picking up his razor.

The servant would not volunteer any information, but now that he was captive, holding the mirror, he might be pressed a little about Suzanne's troubles.

Ben completed a few strokes and made a great play of cleaning the soap from his razor, leaving himself free to speak. "Have you any more news of Bonaparte?" That was a relatively safe question in this royalist household.

"Not yet, sir. He left Lyons the day after you moved in here. There have been rumours aplenty, but we've heard nothing definite."

Ben muttered something incomprehensible and continued to ply the sharp blade. Suzanne had made him extremely comfortable here in Marguerite's bedchamber and had ensured he wanted for nothing. Except, obviously, to hold her in his arms, which was becoming almost an obsession with every minute he spent in her company.

"I'd say Bonaparte must have reached Paris by now." Guillaume paused and grimaced. "Unless he met with some opposition on the way which, I have to tell you, sir, I very much doubt. A turncoat army. Every last man of them."

Ben wiped the razor once more. "Miss Suzanne must be worrying about her sister. Having no news is bound to be unsettling. But pray assure Miss Suzanne, and Madame Grolier, too, that Jacques is a most resourceful man. He will never allow any harm to come to Miss Marguerite."

Guillaume frowned over the top of the mirror but said nothing.

Ben carefully scraped the last bristles from his chin. Soon Guillaume was making ready to leave. "Guillaume, be so good as to ask Miss Suzanne to step up to see me when she has a moment to spare."

Guillaume turned back from the door and glared at Ben. He clearly thought such a request was inappropriate. Ben's conscience agreed, but that would not stop him. "Tell her, if you will," he added quietly, "that I have remembered some information she will wish to be aware of."

Guillaume looked surprised but, after a moment, he nodded and left.

Ben lay back on his pillows and stroked his newly-shaven jaw with his free hand. He hadn't made a very good job of it, but at least he looked less of a fright than he had when his head had been swathed in bandages and his hair had been matted with blood.

He closed his eyes and tried not to think about Suzanne. He failed. His body was definitely recovering now, for the very thought of her delectable person was having a marked effect. He swore. It did not help.

The door opened before he was fully back in control of his body. It was Suzanne. He quickly raised his knees and rearranged the bedclothes. Then he swallowed hard and forced himself to concentrate on his need for information.

"Guillaume thinks that Bonaparte must be in Paris by now. He clearly holds out no hope that King Louis's army will have remained loyal."

She was standing by the open door. Her eyes were cast down. She neither moved nor spoke.

39

"I know that you are troubled," Ben said quickly, filling the awkward silence. "You are bound to be worrying about your sister, but I can assure you that Jacques will defend her. With his life, if needs be." He paused before continuing in a gentler voice, "Has something given you cause for concern?"

Suzanne started back, shocked. "What did Guillaume say about me? He had no right." Spots of high colour flared on her cheeks. She looked as though she were about to rush out of the room, probably to berate Guillaume.

Ben stretched out his left hand to stay her and draw her nearer. "Pray do not blame Guillaume, Suzanne. He did not say anything about you or your sister. Come, sit down. Tell me. I may be useless as far as physical defences are concerned—" he nodded down at his bandages "—but there is nothing wrong with my brain. If there is a problem, and if there is anything that can be done from here in Lyons, we will find a way to do it, I promise you."

Chapter Seven

SUZANNE TOOK A DEEP BREATH and stepped fully into the room, pushing the door behind her. How could she resist that outstretched hand? She longed to take it, to clasp it to her heart, but she did not dare. She might love Benn— and her heart would surely break when he left her—but she would not indulge in a missish gesture that Benn would scorn. Or, worse, that he would pity.

At least he had not blamed her troubled mood on that tiny, betraying touch of their hands over the coffee cup. Let him continue to think she was worrying about her sister.

She raised her chin and looked him in the eye. "Guillaume said you had some information for me?" she began. Then, letting her suspicions show, she added sternly, "And how, pray, have you acquired it when you are confined to bed?"

Benn dropped his gaze for a second. Suzanne fancied that his colour had heightened a fraction, too.

"I have to admit, Suzanne, that I, er, misled you a little. I have no new information. As you rightly say, how could I have, lying here?" He shrugged. A mistake. A shadow of pain crossed his face.

Fear clamped like a vice round Suzanne's heart. She had taken an involuntary step towards him before she managed to stop. She clasped her hands firmly together. She would not allow herself to touch him, even if he was in pain.

41

"Suzanne, we need to talk. Please listen to me. I am...I am concerned for you. You cannot continue to bear your burdens alone. Now that your sister has gone to Paris, you have no one to confide in. I know you would not stoop to share your concerns with mere servants."

Suzanne drew herself up a little more and looked down her nose at him. She doubted that Benn had ever faced the sort of hardships that the Grolier family had endured. Benn might be too haughty to trust "mere servants" but Suzanne and her sister were not. Guillaume had been a rock for their family when more exalted people had deserted them. The Groliers had remained true to their King, at the cost of their family's fortune and status. Benn, as an Englishman, could never understand what the French had suffered through the Reign of Terror and the years of Bonaparte's despotism.

Benn stretched out his hand once more. Then he smiled up at her in a way that touched her heart. She fought down a sudden urge to throw herself on his chest and pour out all her troubles. Such a beguiling smile. Was he really offering to share her burdens?

"You smile, sir. I fancy you do not understand the threats we face. This is France, not England. Traitors, and the innocent as well, are sent to the guillotine in this country. We have had years to learn that trust is not a matter of rank or status. I have trusted my servants with my life. And with *your* life, too."

This time, his blush was unmistakeable. It made him look very young and vulnerable. The white bandages contrasted starkly with his high colour. "I beg your pardon, Miss Suzanne," he said formally, bowing his head a little. "I meant no insult, I promise you. But I see that my words were worse than thoughtless." He gazed up at her, his blue eyes wide and apologetic. "Can you forgive me, my dear?"

Suzanne's heart lurched. How was she to resist when he used such words?

She tried to clear her throat. "Let us forget it," she said a little gruffly, fixing her gaze on the wall above his head.

Benn was, without doubt, the handsomest man she had ever seen. His spare masculine beauty made her pulses race and her thoughts tumble whenever she looked at him. How was she supposed to keep her wits about her when she was near him? No woman could do it.

Wrong. Marguerite did it.

That rebellious little voice was back inside Suzanne's head, reminding her of her strong-minded sister, who was now far away and might be in great danger. Suzanne swallowed the fear that clutched at her throat.

With an obvious effort, Benn forced himself up from his pillows and thrust himself forward to grab Suzanne's hand. He fell back again at once, his weight pulling her with him.

"Ouf." She landed on the edge of the bed in an undignified heap. She opened her mouth to rail at him.

He was too quick for her. He gave her fingers a tiny squeeze, which silenced her completely. She felt as if a torrent of steaming water was enveloping her body, pouring from the fingers that held her own. Her heart lurched.

Oh, Benn. Why do you do this? Why do you inflict this torture on me? She wished she had the courage to speak her thoughts aloud. It was impossible. She clamped her lips tightly together to prevent any rebellious sounds from escaping.

"You are angry with me," he said softly. "And I admit I have given you cause. But my motives are of the best. I beg you to believe that." He squeezed her hand again. When she did not object—for she still could not speak—Benn's smile returned, then widened. "You may think me only a dunderheaded Englishman who understands nothing of French hardships. And you would be right, at least in part. But what I *do* understand, Suzanne, is you. You have nursed me for long enough now that I know your ways, your gentleness, your healing touch. I see the kindness in your face when you come to tend me. I see other emotions, too."

Suzanne closed her eyes against his words.

"This morning," he continued, almost without a pause, "I could see how troubled you were. You almost fled from this room. What happened to our companionable conversations after morning coffee?" He grinned teasingly at her. "Why, you did not even remember to take away the empty cups. Guillaume had to do it later. As if he did not already have enough chores," he added, in a voice of mock reproof. "Shame on you, Miss."

She raised her head, slowly, to look at him. Ben saw that her eyes were huge and sheened with tears. That hurt. He felt as if he had been struck a blow. And with justice. This remarkable girl was bearing the burdens of her whole family. No wonder she could not respond to his silly teasing. He should be taking her in his arms, stroking her hair and soothing her with sympathetic words. She needed comfort and gentle caresses. But he did not even have two good arms to offer her. He—

Driven by his overwhelming need to console her, Ben stopped trying to think. He acted on pure instinct, and surprised himself by doing something totally foreign to him. Keeping his gaze locked with hers, he lifted her hand to his lips and kissed it. Her eyes widened even more. He heard her sharp intake of breath, impossibly loud in the stunned silence. She sat motionless, like a radiant statue wrought from glowing, pink-tinged marble. She was so beautiful that it almost pained him to look on her, knowing that they had only a few more days together and that he would never set eyes on her again once he left this place.

Slowly and very deliberately, Ben turned her hand in his and put his lips to her tender palm.

It was as if the marble had been touched by the finger of some ancient god and brought instantly to life. Her whole body shuddered. She moaned deep in her throat. And her glorious eyes, darkening to almost black, closed against his gaze.

What was he doing to this poor girl? Ben knew he should have been feeling compassion, along with proper remorse for treating Suzanne in such a cavalier fashion. He felt neither. His whole body was exultant that she should respond to him so. Hard, masculine pride surged through him. What he was feeling for Suzanne Grolier was sheer, unquenchable desire. And he was beginning to suspect that she might be feeling it, too.

For long minutes, neither of them moved. Ben feasted his gaze on her, seeing for the first time how the tiny tendrils of fine fair hair escaped to curl at her temples and caress her porcelain skin. Her eyelashes were thick and surprisingly dark. They rested on her blushing cheeks like downy feathers, waiting to be blown away by the whim of the breeze—or by the breath of a lover's kiss. Ben raised his lips from her palm and strained forward, as if drawn by an invisible thread. He was going to kiss—

Her eyes flew open. She was shocked. Her lips worked as if she were saying his name, but there was no sound. And then she turned her head away.

It was over. The thread was broken. Ben gently returned her hand to her lap, resisting the temptation to allow himself a last caress. His body was now raging with desire. If Suzanne were aware of even half of what he was feeling, she would flee from him in horror. She was an innocent girl, untutored in the base lusts of men.

"Tell me what happened today, Suzanne. Why are you so upset?" When she said nothing, Ben knew it was time to insist. "Has something happened to your mother?"

They were interrupted by a soft tap on the door.

"Yes? Who is there?" Suzanne's voice sounded hoarse and strained.

"It is I, mistress," said the voice of Guillaume. "Pray come. I have something you need to see."

Suzanne wiped a shaky hand across her mouth and rose, smoothing her skirts. A moment later, she was gone and the door was firmly closed between them.

Alone in the silence, Ben collapsed back onto his pillows and groaned out his frustrations to the empty room.

45

• • • •

Guillaume's hands were empty. He looked a bit furtive. He glanced sideways towards Marguerite's bedchamber door. He appeared to be listening for something.

"What do you want, Guillaume?" Suzanne asked impatiently.

He put a finger to his lips and ushered her into her own room, motioning to her to close the door.

Mystified, she obeyed, but she was beginning to be annoyed by his behaviour. "What is it? You—"

"Hush. Not so loud, mistress. He—" Guillaume jerked a thumb in the direction of the connecting door to the silk store "—he must not hear."

Suzanne ignored the implications of that, but she did lower her voice. "What is it that I should see, Guillaume?"

He slid his fingers inside his leather jerkin and pulled out a small packet.

Suzanne's breath caught. It looked like a letter. From her sister? Eagerly, she snatched it from the servant's fingers.

"Slowly, mistress. Look carefully at what you have there."

"What?" Then she saw. It was indeed a letter. The handwriting was Marguerite's. And the seal had already been broken.

Chapter Eight

BEN'S BODY WAS MORE OR LESS under control again when there was another knock on his door. It would be Guillaume. After what had happened between them earlier, Suzanne would probably never enter this room again.

Before Ben could say a word, the door was thrown open. It was Suzanne.

She stood on the threshold for a moment, wide-eyed and staring. She was very pale. Then she shook her head, as if admonishing herself, and came over to the bed. She stood there, tense and still, looking down at him.

Ben held his breath, afraid to move or speak. And then she crumpled on to the bed. Her shoulders slumped, her hands went to cover her face, and soon her whole body was shaking with convulsive sobs.

Ben reached out his hand, but let it drop again before it could touch her shoulder. She needed his advice and counsel. Feeding his rampaging lust even further would be of no help at all.

Her weeping stopped almost at once. She began fumbling in her pocket. Ben reached under his pillow for his own clean handkerchief and pushed it into her fingers.

She raised her head, surprised. "Thank you." Her voice was barely a whisper. She wiped her reddened eyes and then blew her nose hard. She had begun to shake her head, in disbelief at her own weakness, Ben decided. Or was it in rejection of him?

She straightened her shoulders and looked at Ben. The handkerchief was a screwed-up ball in her clenched fingers. "We are lost," she began in a small, lifeless voice. "Marguerite sent back the trunk of silks from Paris since she could not sell any there. The trunk was broken open on the way."

"The silks have been stolen?" Ben knew that Marguerite had taken almost half their stock. He could guess at the damage such a loss would do. The family needed every *sou* that the sale of their wares could bring. Marguerite had surely been foolhardy to entrust her silks to a carrier in such dangerous times.

"No. Nothing is missing."

"I'm afraid I don't understand." He frowned a little and would have touched her if he dared, to show her the depth of his concern. But that was out of the question, for his body would go up in flames.

"No, how could you?" She sounded strange, distant, as if she were talking to someone else, someone invisible. "The trunk has two keys. Marguerite carries one when she travels. The other is kept here. That way, if the trunk must be sent by carrier, we can be sure that its contents have not been tampered with."

This was all extremely odd. Had she not said, barely a moment ago, that none of the precious fabrics had been stolen?

Before he could say a word, Suzanne continued in that same thready voice, "They broke open the trunk, but they took nothing. What they wanted was Marguerite's letter. They broke into that, too."

Ben's heart began to beat very fast. Now he *did* understand. Suzanne must have seen the shadow of the guillotine over them all. No wonder she sounded odd. She must be terrified. And what on earth had possessed Marguerite to enclose a letter? What was Jack about, to allow her to do such a thing? Such indiscretion could be the death of them all. They would—

He was beginning to panic, too. But then his logical mind reasserted itself. There was a strange mystery here. "How do you know there was a letter, Suzanne?"

Her hand went to the bosom of her plain muslin gown. "It was still in the trunk. But the seal was broken." She swallowed and raised her chin defiantly. "I have sent the boy to hire a horse so that you, at least, can escape. Guillaume will help you to make ready. And once you are gone, we will simply deny all their accusations." She sounded stronger, but resigned. Clearly, she did not believe denials would achieve much.

Ben's logical mind was now running at top speed. He could instantly see the flaws in her reasoning, even if poor Suzanne could not. He smiled reassuringly at her. "How long is it since the trunk arrived in the city?"

"What? What does that matter? You are in danger, Benn. We all are. You must leave. *Now*." She was wringing her hands and there was panic in her eyes.

Ben resisted the temptation to stroke the trouble from her hands. Slowly, and very calmly, he repeated his question.

She frowned, but this time she did answer. "Oh, several hours, I suppose. The trunk would have arrived at the coach office some time yesterday, but it was not delivered until half an hour ago. I don't see that the timing changes anything." She had overcome her despair now, and was sounding much more like her normal self. And she was clearly irritated that he had not immediately jumped to do her bidding.

"It changes everything, my dear Suzanne," Ben said firmly. "If Bonaparte's agents were going to arrest us all, they would have done so by now. 'Strike while the iron is hot' as the proverb goes. And why would they have left you the letter, knowing that you would understand the danger as soon as you saw the broken seal? No, trust me when I tell you that they will not come."

Her eyes widened, and she clasped her hands together. Then her mouth opened just enough to allow the tip of her tongue to moisten her lower lip. Ben recognised it for an unconscious gesture, born of anxiety, but the effect on him was electrifying. It was the most sensuous move he had ever seen. Desire flooded through him, all over again.

Suzanne seemed to notice nothing. "But it *must* have been Bonaparte's agents," she protested. "Thieves would have stolen the silk and ignored the letter."

Ben forced himself to respond to her words and not to her distress. "You are right about the thieves. And you are right to assume that Bonaparte's men broke into your trunk and read your sister's letter. Then they were arrogant enough to send you both trunk and letter. They want you to know what they have done."

"So they *do* suspect us. Benn, you must—"

"Do not panic. I'm sure there is no need. I'd say it is more likely that they want to display their power. They want you and all the people of Lyons to be afraid. They know there are royalists in this city, so they are sending a very clear message—everyone is a suspect, everyone's possessions can be searched at will, and no one is safe under Bonaparte's law." Suzanne's pale skin was turning ashen at his words. "But in this case, your sister's letter has passed their test. I am sure that must be so, Suzanne, or they would have been here in the night to arrest us. Tell me, what did she say?" He had convinced himself, by his own hard logic. But could he convince poor doubting Suzanne?

She began to speak, but she soon faltered. Taking a deep breath, she straightened her shoulders and drew a folded paper out of her bodice. "I think it is best if you read it for yourself. I assumed we were all betrayed. Perhaps you can assure me that I am wrong? I hope so. I hope so very much."

Ben took the letter and unfolded it carefully. The paper was still warm from its contact with Suzanne's body. There was the faintest scent of the lavender in which she stored her clothes. It lingered in the back of Ben's throat like the perfume of the finest wine. And one mouthful was not nearly enough.

Ben tried to concentrate on the letter. It was short. And it was very cleverly crafted. Had Suzanne been so shocked by the broken seal that she had failed to notice that? Marguerite had given nothing away, not even her own name, but there were hidden messages here, nevertheless. She was going to visit someone she referred to as "the curé." She mentioned the possibility of a visit to the coast. What did she mean by these tantalising references? Was she planning to help Jack to escape to England? Ben could see no other explanation.

"Who is the curé your sister speaks of? Do you know where he lives? She says that is where she is going. She makes no mention at all of Jacques, but I assume that he will go with her."

Ben's factual questions seemed to restore Suzanne's normal poise. "I am not sure… A curé living by the coast? I… Oh, I remember. Marguerite and I were only children, but there was a curé, Father Bertrand, who, er, who knew our family well in the old days. The poor man had to leave Lyons during the troubles. I think Guillaume mentioned once that he went to Normandy. A village somewhere near Rouen, he said."

"Ah. I see." The tension began to leave Ben's shoulders. "Your sister is a brave and resourceful woman, Suzanne. She is telling us, through this subtly coded letter, that she and Jacques are making for the coast so that he can take ship for England." He grinned at her, feeling more than a little smug at having deciphered Marguerite's code where Suzanne could not.

"But why on earth should he do that? Jacques should be here. His place is alongside his fellow royalists, fighting for our cause. You must return to England, Benn, but you are English. Jacques is a Frenchman."

51

Ben knew, in that instant, that his face had given him away.

"What? No. Oh, dear God!" Suzanne exclaimed. "Your friend Jacques is another English spy. You gulled us all." She was so furious, she seemed to be about to strike him. "You...you blackguard!" she spat instead, her voice full of loathing.

There was no point in denying it. "You are right," he conceded, trying to keep his tone light. "The only difference between us is that he can pass for a Frenchman, and I cannot. Jacques... His mother is French, you see. It's actually Jack," he added, with a rueful smile as he changed the pronunciation of his friend's name.

His attempts to charm her did not seem to be working.

She glared at him, disgusted. "And 'Jack' is his real name." It was not a question.

Ben did not reply, for he would not lie to her. But he had told Suzanne quite enough now. It would be dangerous for her to learn more.

Her next question surprised him. "But what about Marguerite? Her English spy—this two-faced Jack of yours—will abandon her and sail back to his own country. She will be left alone, and in danger. Oh, war is cruel to treat poor women so. And English spies are heartless." She rose and turned her back on him, hurrying for the door.

"Don't go. Please, Suzanne." The words were out before he knew it. He took a deep breath, fixing his gaze on her straight, tense back. "Jack is an honourable man, Suzanne. He knows how much he owes...how much we both owe to you and your sister. I know he will ensure that Marguerite is safe before he leaves. If not with the curé, then somewhere else. He would never abandon her. As I could never abandon you."

She spun on her heel to confront him. But it was no true confrontation. Her face was more flushed than he had ever seen it. Her eyes were sparkling with unshed tears. Ben fancied that her hands were shaking.

"Never?" Her voice was shaking, too.

For a heartbeat, their eyes locked as Ben struggled to catch the thoughts tumbling round in his brain. What he had said was true—about Jack, certainly. And about himself? Had he intended to make such a promise to Suzanne? He did not know. And now she was staring at him, waiting for him to turn that hasty pledge into…into something more. But what? He opened his mouth to speak, but no words came out. He was floundering. He swallowed hard. Once, and then again. Still no words.

Suzanne was watching—and reading—his every move. And she was clearly reading rejection. She turned and fled from the room.

Chapter Nine

THERE WAS NO GOING BACK. He must continue with his mission—he had no choice there—but he was now bound to Suzanne Grolier by ties of honour. Somehow, he would have to find a way of ensuring her future safety and her comfort. That was not what he really wanted. What he really wanted was to take her in his arms, to feel her lithe, strong body under his own, to show her what passion could be between a man and a woman.

It was out of the question. He knew that. She was no loose woman, but a solid *bourgeoise*, the daughter of an honest trader. She was not of Ben's class, but she was not of a class that he could trifle with, either. It would be dishonourable for Ben to seduce any girl of the *bourgeoisie*. With Suzanne, it would be even more unthinkable, for he had now pledged himself to protect her.

He should think of her as a sister.

That made him laugh out loud, so much so that a shaft of pain tore through his wounded shoulder, a telling reminder of the risks he ran by acting without careful thought. Before leaving for Paris, Jack had been rash enough to swear on the Grolier family bible that he would treat Marguerite as a sister. What a battle—honour versus desire. Ben wondered whether Jack was managing to resist the temptation that Marguerite most certainly presented. She would make a luscious armful and, unlike Ben, Jack had two good arms to wrap around her.

Ben tried to push that sensuous image from his mind. Lying here, in the absent Marguerite's room, injured and idle, was doing him no good at all. He needed something to do—to keep his mind busy and away from lustful imaginings.

He would make a start, right now, by getting back on to his feet.

• • • •

Suzanne was refusing to think about what Benn had said. She told herself she had far too much to do, finishing her accounts and sorting out the precious fabrics from Marguerite's trunk. She was glad she had asked for Guillaume's help with that. Although he said little, his company was comforting.

She piled the last of the parcels into his arms. "Take these upstairs, please, Guillaume, and stack them behind the door. I will lay them out properly when I have finished with the accounts."

"I shall need the storeroom key."

Suzanne picked up the bunch of keys from the office desk, removed the one for the little door on the landing and dropped it into Guillaume's pocket. "Try not to make too much noise, please. Remember there is only a thin partition between the silk store and Marguerite's chamber. Our, er, guest may be trying to sleep."

"As you say, mistress." Guillaume left, carrying his load. Was he going to heed her instructions? There was no way of knowing.

Suzanne sat down behind the desk and tried to concentrate on the column of figures she had been adding up. Guillaume would be in the silk store by now, only feet from where Benn lay. If she had taken the silk upstairs herself, instead of sending the old manservant, she could have unlocked the connecting door between the silk store and Benn's room. She could have gazed at his beautiful sleeping body. If he were awake, she could even have spoken to him. She could have —

Spoken to him? What on earth could she have said? *Pray, sir, what did you mean when you said you would never abandon me? And how long is "never"?*

55

She threw down her pen. Whatever Benn had meant by those hasty words, it certainly would not include either love or marriage. Had he perhaps been thinking of the danger they were all in and of the debt he owed to the Grolier sisters for sheltering two English spies? Once Bonaparte was finally defeated—for that blessed day would surely come—there would no longer be any need for protection. The English spies would return to their comfortable life. And the Grolier sisters would return to their daily grind at the loom.

She stared down at her desk. Even the simple figures in her ledger seemed to be tinged with gloom, as if a fine grey gauze had been thrown over everything. The future that stretched before her was far from appealing. She knew she would probably end her days as a worn-out old spinster who had never known the joys of marriage and children, a dried-up husk who had never been loved.

Your future is your own to decide, Suzanne.

Her inner voice was back. And at the most inconvenient time. She did not wish to be reminded of all that she had lost.

Marriage and children may not be for you to decide, but love can be sought and found in other ways. Your future lies in your own hands.

Suzanne jumped to her feet and began to pace. She allowed herself the indulgence of a few choice curses, though only under her breath. They helped to drown out the sound of that inner voice. It was tormenting her, sketching a tantalising vision of things she could never have. Still, *one* thing was true. She was mistress of her own life. And although the Groliers had lost land and status in the Revolution, they had not lost everything. Unlike some, Suzanne had not been reduced to abject poverty. She knew she had much to be thankful for. She might have been forced into menial service—or worse.

She took a deep breath and smiled round at the silent room. It was functional, but comfortable. In Marguerite's

56

absence, Suzanne ruled here. She could make her own decisions. She would choose to ignore Benn's strange promise. Since he would not be with her for much longer, she would live every second of the time they had left. *To the full.*

Once he was gone from her, she would have only memories. She was free to choose to make those memories the sweetest they could possibly be. And she would. She would show him a smiling face and a glad heart, and she would live for the moment, no matter what he said or what he did.

Still smiling, she sat down once more and picked up her pen. In her new and composed state of mind, even the columns of figures did not dare to rebel.

• • • •

Days and days of hard, painful effort had made a difference to Ben's physical state. His shoulder was still not fully healed, but he was now able to use his right arm quite a lot, though only with caution. His muscles were still weak and sudden movements could be very painful. Still, the bandages would soon be removed for good and he would eventually be almost back to normal. Unfortunately, that also meant that Suzanne would cease to visit him here in his bedchamber.

To be honest, she should have stopped doing so already, in fulfilment of a promise to her sister. She had agreed not to spend time alone in Ben's chamber once he was back on his feet. Which he now was. Ben was proud that Suzanne had shared that confidence with him, but he had not been equally frank with her. In fact, he had taken the greatest care to hide the truth. As far as Suzanne knew, he was mending remarkably slowly and was still much too weak to rise from his bed.

A minor deception, Ben assured himself. For a very good cause.

It was not that he was about to break his pledge to ensure Suzanne's future. He was determined not to fail her there. Nor did he plan to take advantage of her during their short times alone together. That would be the work of an utter scoundrel. No, it was more that those times with her had become so very precious of late. He still revelled in the touch of her hands on his skin, but he had also learned to appreciate her sharp brain and her lively sense of fun. Scarcely a day passed without gales of laughter filling his bedchamber. That had helped him to forget the dangers surrounding them all. He knew he would treasure those moments once he had left her, and was far from Lyons.

That would be all too soon.

• • • •

"Mistress!" Guillaume burst into the office without bothering to knock. His face was full of alarm.

Suzanne rose quietly to her feet, doing her best to disguise her concern. She was in charge of this little household. It was her duty to remain calm and businesslike. "Goodness, Guillaume," she said, a little testily, "since when have you forgotten how to knock?"

He stopped short. His weather-beaten skin could not conceal the colour that flooded into his face. It was a very long time since he had had to be reprimanded by anyone. Whatever his news, it must be important.

"What has happened?" she asked, a bit more encouragingly.

"Mistress, I must warn you that the house is being watched."

Suzanne's breath caught in her throat, but she managed to keep silent.

"One of Bonaparte's agents is lurking on the other side of the street, two houses down."

"But how do you know he's an agent?" she choked out.

Guillaume smiled grimly. "He's become very free with his opinions since we heard the news of Bonaparte's triumphant entry into Paris. I suspected him before, I may tell you, but now there's no doubt. He's watching our street. And he may be watching our house. We can't be sure, but it's best to assume the worst."

Suzanne looked over her shoulder towards the window. "Can I see him from here? It would be best if I knew exactly what the enemy looks like."

Guillaume nodded. "I knew you would not be afraid to fight, mistress." Then, as Suzanne started for the window, he said, "You'd be best to look from Miss Marguerite's window, upstairs. He's unlikely to be watching the upper storeys. If you look from here, he may see you and realise he's been rumbled. We don't want to risk that. They might replace him with someone we don't recognise."

Suzanne grinned at the servant. "You are a fine old schemer, Guillaume. I am glad that we are fighting on the same side."

He shrugged. "I only wish we knew more of what the Bonapartists are plotting. That way, we might be able to forestall them."

"Well…" Suzanne paused, thinking. To her surprise, she was not afraid. She felt as if her blood was all afire. If she had been a man, she would have been buckling on her sword for the coming battle. But she was only a woman, so she would have to find another way. "Tell me, Guillaume, do Bonaparte's agents know where your sympathies lie?"

"No, of course not."

"Forgive me for seeming to doubt you. I had to be sure. Now, are you prepared for a little spying on your own account?" When he nodded, she smiled broadly and told him exactly what she wanted him to do.

• • • •

Suzanne was humming to herself as she raced up to Marguerite's room. Guillaume had provided her with the perfect excuse for visiting Benn, though she had no intention of telling him that the house was being watched. Such disturbing news would merely serve to frustrate him. Poor man. It was taking such a long time for his wounds to heal.

She reached the door and raised her hand to knock. What if he was asleep? She put her ear to the door. Nothing.

There was another way. Taking her keys from her pocket, she unlocked the door to the silk store that had been created in the gap between the walls of Marguerite's bedchamber and her own. There was no window inside, and she had not thought to light a candle so early in the evening. So she unlocked the connecting door that led from the store into her own bedchamber and threw it wide. Light flooded in. A stray beam caught some fine red silk shot with silver, making it glitter like a spider's web hung with dew. She could not prevent a little smile of satisfaction at the sight. She had woven that silk with her own hands.

• • • •

Ben forced himself to move stealthily back from the window. A man watching the house. Ben clenched an impotent fist and cursed under his breath. He had to do something. But what?

Racking his brains, he went back to walking quietly up and down between the bed and the window. The house was safe enough for the moment. He was sure he could not be seen from the street below and, as always, he was taking care to step softly so that no one in the house would suspect that he was on his feet. Regular exercise was making his legs almost as strong as before; his upper body was improving, too, though his right arm still hurt abominably whenever he raised it above his shoulder or tried to grip. He was certainly in no condition to fight.

If he warned the household about the watcher, Suzanne would discover that he was much, much better than he pretended. She would know he had deceived her.

But he could not keep quiet if Suzanne was in danger. Surely there was *something* he could do?

He could enlist Guillaume's help, though he doubted that even two of them together could deal with this danger. The watcher opposite might appear to be alone, but there were bound to be others, probably quite close. In a busy city street, a pistol shot would be worse than useless. They could try kidnapping the man, but that might bring even more of Bonaparte's agents down on them. They might start to search from house to house.

No, the only solution was to watch and wait. There were many houses packed into this street. The man could be watching any of them. No need to terrify Suzanne's household by warning them too soon. Ben simply had to ensure that nothing happened to draw the watcher's attention on to the Grolier house.

He risked one more glance into the street. The watcher was still there, but making no effort at concealment. Perhaps he was not a spy after all? Ben shook his head at his own naivety and continued with his furtive exercise program. It was safest to assume that the watcher was a spy unless there was proof that he was not.

A slight noise startled him, breaking his train of thought. Was someone there? He was safe enough, he knew, for he had locked his door before starting his exercises. He would tell his visitor to return later, by which time he would be safely back in his bed, to all appearances still an invalid.

· · · ·

Suzanne was still smiling as she relocked the door to the landing and turned to unlock the connecting door to Benn's bedchamber. First, she listened again. This time, she fancied she could hear some kind of movement, but it was strangely muffled. He must be awake, but what on earth could he be doing? If she opened the door, would she see something that would embarrass them both?

Taking care to make no noise, she inserted the key into the lock. She hesitated. Did she dare?

Of course she did. Their house was being watched by the enemy. They might all be arrested at any moment. She and Benn might never have another chance to be alone together. Compared with that, what was the risk of a little embarrassment?

She turned the key, rapped a quick warning knock on the wood and opened the door a little way. "Forgive me, Benn, I—" She took one step into the room and stopped dead. "Why, you—" She felt the blood rushing to her face. "You...you charlatan. You wicked trickster. There is nothing wrong with you at all."

Benn had gulled her, yet again.

He was not lying in his bed, still weak and suffering, as she had expected. He was not even struggling to get back on his feet. He was fully upright, wrapped only in a skimpy sheet, and padding very softly up and down his bedchamber. As he walked, barefoot, he was stretching and flexing the muscles of his injured shoulder and arm. Suzanne's carefully applied bandages and the sling she had fashioned were hanging loose against his naked torso.

He had played her for a fool. First he had led her to believe that Mr Jacques was a Frenchman; and now he was pretending to be a bed-ridden invalid when he was nothing of the sort. What else was he capable of? Were all those kind words mere flirtation, to divert her from asking questions about what he was really doing? And those touches of the hand, those caresses... Did they mean nothing at all?

She took a deep breath. This time, she would not be diverted. This time, she would tell him exactly what she thought of him.

Chapter Ten

BEN WAS SHOCKED TO SEE the locked door in the middle of the side wall swing open. It had never been used before and he had assumed it never would be. Foolish to make assumptions, for now he was caught by his own lack of foresight.

Suzanne stepped into the room, and seemed to take in the whole situation at a glance. Her face instantly became flushed with anger, overlaid with humiliation at the way she had been deceived. He could not blame her.

"You charlatan. You wicked trickster!" she raged. "There is nothing wrong with you at all."

Her voice was rising with every accusation. Ben knew she had to be stopped before the sound reached the street and aroused the suspicions of the watcher below.

"And to think that I felt sorry for you, that I was worrying about why it was taking so long for your wound to heal. You were laughing at me all the time, weren't you? Oh, you...you... You are beneath contempt."

He did not hesitate any longer. She had now given him the best possible excuse for yielding to his baser instincts. He pulled her against his body and stopped her mouth with a long, hard kiss.

She squirmed against him, trying to free herself, but without success. Ben might be far from fully fit, but he was still much stronger than Suzanne. He was certain that she was not afraid, however. She was much too angry for that.

He could not stop kissing her. It was heaven.

He wrapped his arms more tightly around her body, ignoring the pain that stabbed into his shoulder. It was well worth the pain to hold her. The warmth of her glorious body against his bare skin was sheer delight, as was the subtle scent of lavender on her clothes and in her pale gold curls.

"Mmm." A groan of pure pleasure escaped him before he could swallow it.

That sound had a strange effect on Suzanne. First, she stopped trying to break free, and then she slid her arms around Ben's waist. What had been anger seemed to be turning into desire. Instead of fighting his kiss, she was returning it, and with more innocent passion than Ben would have dreamt possible.

He groaned again, as he gentled and then deepened the kiss. He had never known anything like this. It was as if he were drowning. Everything else was forgotten, everything except his driving need to taste her luscious mouth and to show her the pleasure that mutual passion could bring.

When he touched the tip of his tongue to the tender flesh inside her bottom lip, he felt a great shudder run through her whole body. She reached up to put her arms around his neck and pull his mouth even closer to hers.

"Argh!" Ben's cry of pain was swallowed in Suzanne's kiss, but it broke the spell of their mindless desire. They pulled apart, both gasping for breath and beginning to gabble apologies.

"I hurt you. I'm sorry, I—"

"I'm sorry, I should not have—"

They stopped in the same moment. And then Suzanne began to laugh, a joyous sound that somehow reminded Ben of pealing bells under a perfect blue sky. The image in his mind was perfection. Just like Suzanne.

Ben touched a finger to her cheek. Her eyes widened. Her laughter died away, leaving her lips curved in a knowing smile.

"Forgive me," he said quietly. "I should not have done that. But you were starting to scream at me and I had to stop you. There is a man down below, watching—"

"How did you find out?" she exclaimed sharply. Her smile had vanished.

Ben eased his left arm round her shoulders and began to stroke the top of her arm. She did not resist. She even leaned towards him, as the tension began to leave her. "I am a spy," he said. "It's my business to keep watch."

"Even when you're supposed to be too ill to rise from your bed?"

"Even then." He dropped a gentle kiss on her forehead and let her go. Then he crossed to the window and carefully glanced out. "He has gone. The danger is over for now. But I do apologise for having deceived you. I assure you I meant no harm."

"What you *meant,* sir, was to entice me into your lair, to get me into your power so that you could...you could..."

"So that I could...?" He grinned wickedly at her.

"Oh, you are a wretch, Benn. You know perfectly well what I mean. You simply wish to put me to the blush." She put her hands to her hot cheeks.

While what she said was perfectly true, she was completely ignoring the most obviously improper aspect of this strange tête-à-tête—that Ben was wearing nothing but a thin folded sheet, tied around his middle. He ought to ask her to leave so that he could make himself decent, but after that mind-shattering kiss, he was quite incapable of letting her go. If she could treat a nearly naked man as if she were meeting him in a drawing room, who was he to object?

"I apologise, Suzanne. I shall now attempt to make amends by changing the subject. Tell me about your silk store. I presume that is where this door leads? I did try it several times, but it was always locked."

"Naturally. It would have been improper to have it otherwise, since there is another door on the far side which leads straight into my bedchamber." She pulled the door wide. "See?"

The silk store was a dark, narrow room, little more than a wide corridor. Immediately opposite the door into Ben's room was another. It stood wide open, letting in the light from the bedchamber beyond. Ben could see the end of a bed, and a delicate lace-edged bedgown lying across it. He tried not to imagine how Suzanne would look when she was wearing it, but it was all too real. The fabric was as thin as gauze.

Goaded, Ben marched smartly into the store and pulled Suzanne's door closed. He was suffering enough temptation already, with Suzanne standing beside him, even though she was fully clothed.

When he returned to his room, she was frowning at him. "I thought you were interested in our silk."

"I was. I am. But with my door open, there is more than enough light. Will you show me the wonders you have created? I would welcome a chance to admire your skill before I leave Lyons."

Her expression froze for a second, but then she smiled brightly at him. "It will be my pleasure," she said in a brittle voice. "Though some of the work is Marguerite's, not mine."

Ben stood back to let Suzanne precede him into the silk store. Her walk was unconsciously alluring. He found he could not take his eyes from the seductive sway of her hips. The folds of her light muslin skirt were opening and closing with a hypnotic rhythm, like an oyster responding to the ebb and flow of incoming waves. This oyster concealed a pearl, for she was a pearl of a girl. She should be gowned in silk and lace, not workaday muslin, he decided. Her lustrous beauty should shine against a backdrop of the finest fabrics.

He followed her into the depths of the silk store. In seconds, he found he was shivering.

She turned at that moment. "Oh, how stupid of me," she exclaimed. "It is cold in here and you have nothing to keep off the chill." She looked round the storeroom, but there were neither blankets nor shawls, only the finest silk and velvet. She allowed a tiny smile to tug at the corner of her mouth as she reached for a bolt of dark blue velvet. With a practised flick of the wrist, she unrolled the sumptuous cloth. "That will do, I fancy. Light as a feather, and warm enough. Also delicate enough to ensure that no weight will fall on your poor wounded shoulder," she added, with a note of sarcasm in her voice.

Without giving Ben a chance to object, she slipped behind him and draped the velvet around his body like a cloak.

She was right. The velvet slithered across his skin like a caress, yet it weighed no more than gossamer. But it was much too beautiful for a man to wear, especially a man hung with coarse bandages.

Suzanne stepped round in front of Ben to assess the effect. "You should have a lighter blue, I think." She cocked her head to one side. "Something closer to the colour of your eyes." She gazed round at the stored fabrics, but all the velvets were of rich, deep colours. She sighed. "A pity." Then her face lit up. "Perhaps a contrast is what we need," she said, with a distinct laugh in her voice. "I wonder…"

Ben watched, bemused, while she selected a deep red silk from the shelf by the door. She whisked the velvet from his shoulders. Then the useless bandages were plucked away and dropped on to the floor. "Raise your arms, if you please." She could have been a mantua-maker, giving a fitting to a lady customer.

Ben wanted to laugh. What on earth would this amazing girl do next?

She surprised him yet again. She began to wind the silk tightly round and round his body so that it covered him from chest to thigh. He was no longer at risk of shivering.

He was now much, much too hot. The evidence of that was embarrassingly plain, in spite of the layers of sheet he still wore next to his skin. The outline of his erection was blatant, painted in the bright accents and dark shadows of rippling red silk. Oh, the woman was a witch. But it was what she wanted. He could not deny her. He remained motionless, waiting.

Suzanne looked at her handiwork and laughed softly, deep in her throat. The temptation had been overwhelming. And the result was more than satisfying. Indeed, it was splendid.

She allowed her gaze to roam over her captive's body. The pale skin of his muscled shoulders was still marred by fading bruises and the ugly healing scar of his wound. Apart from that, he was beautiful. The gleaming silk emphasised the strong lines of his chest. Lower down, she had pulled the fabric taut to show off his narrow waist and hips. The additional effects there were unintended, but altogether delightful to behold, even for a girl who lacked first hand knowledge of the ways of desire.

She chuckled again, wondering whether Benn had any idea of quite how irresistible he looked. At that moment, the light changed. Perhaps the clouds had parted? Whatever the cause, Suzanne would have been ready to swear that there was white lightning forking around Benn's erection, rather than common silver threads.

She took a step towards him and brushed the back of her index finger along that straining ridge. His sharp intake of breath urged her on. She smoothed both her hands slowly around his middle, from his navel to the small of his back, and then down over the swell of his buttocks. It seemed he could not move. He groaned out her name.

The sound shivered all the way down to her toes. If she continued now, there could be no going back.

She did not hesitate. She leaned in to him and pressed her body along the length of his. She could feel the sparks jumping between them; the lightning was piercing her, too. Deep in her belly, there was now a hot, melting ache

"Oh, God, Suzanne. I cannot—"

"Hush." She stopped his protest with a long, drugging kiss. She could not tell him that she loved him. Not in words. Her kisses would have to speak for her.

It seemed they had. Benn's fingers were already at the back of her gown, seeking to undo it. A bubble of laughter began welling up inside her. Had he been too busy spying to notice that modern gowns fastened at the front?

"Ouch." He had caught his finger on a pin. Automatically, he pulled away from her and put his finger to his mouth.

Suzanne gave her laughter free rein for a second, but Benn did not join in. Did he think she was laughing at him? She reached for his hand. Yes, there was a tiny crop of scarlet on the tip of his ring finger. "We cannot risk this on the silk," she murmured, carrying it to her lips. His blood tasted sweet on her tongue. She sucked again, then nipped his skin with her teeth.

His whole body tensed and he drew in a long shaky breath. It took him a moment to speak and, when he did, he voice was tighter and higher than normal. "You are...you are entrancing," he managed at last.

Suzanne placed his hands on the front of her bodice. Then she closed her eyes. She wanted to glory in the touch of his fingers as he undressed her. She wanted to picture it in her mind's eye, as if she were watching his every move through a mirror. He was slow and deliberate, carefully removing every pin and smoothing out every tie. She swayed a little when her petticoats joined her gown in a heap of froth around her feet.

He took both her hands in his. "Will it please you to step out of your muslins, lady?"

Suzanne smiled dreamily. She had no need to see, for she trusted the hands that supported her. She took two steps forward. Apart from her stockings, she was now wearing only her stays over a fine lawn chemise. If she opened her eyes now, if she saw how he was looking at her, she would probably blush to the roots of her hair. Better, much better, to remain in comforting darkness.

He stumbled backwards against a shelf of fabrics. Bolts of cloth began to roll on to the floor. Startled, Suzanne opened her eyes. Hampered by the tight silk around his body, Benn was trying, and failing, to catch the precious materials before they landed. He was muttering under his breath. English curses, she supposed, glad that she could not make out the words.

She crouched down quickly and began to gather up her fallen treasures. There was little harm done. The floor was clean.

"Forgive me, Suzanne. My confounded clumsiness. It always catches me out, especially when I most want to appear in control."

She lifted her head just enough to gaze up at him through her lashes. She hoped she looked as seductive as she intended. "You wish to be in control now?"

"Yes."

"Of yourself?" She waited for a beat. "Or of me?"

His only response was a deep groan.

Suzanne rose. It took only seconds to restore the fabrics to their places. She picked up the cutting shears from the end of the lowest shelf and offered them to Benn. Her stay-laces could only be loosened by nimble fingers, which Benn clearly did not have. And, in any case, it would take much too long. The ache in her belly was urgent.

He was staring at the scissors in his hand as if he had never held such an implement before.

Suzanne put her fingers over his. She leaned forward so that the bare skin of her throat and upper bosom was touching his chest above the red silk. "I need you to see all of me, Benn," she whispered, offering him her lips once again.

He seized her and began to kiss her even more passionately than before. He sucked at her lower lip, then bit it gently before sucking again. Slowly, he brushed the tip of his tongue along the full length of her lips. He pushed into her mouth, tentatively at first, and then with thrusts of increasing desire. He was pulling her body so tight against his own that the cold steel of the scissors was crushed into her flesh. Suzanne did not care. She was being held, being kissed, by the man who had captured her heart. Very soon, he would take her body and make her fully his. She wanted only that.

The scissors must have stabbed him, for he pulled away abruptly. Suzanne's gaze was drawn to his eyes, so wide and dark with passion that there was almost no trace of blue. His lips were parted, and swollen, as hers must also be. They desired each other equally. It was perfect.

Chapter Eleven

SHE HAD PLACED THE SCISSORS in his hands. She wanted him to use them. She wanted him to free her of the remainder of her clothing, to feast his eyes on her body and to use his clumsy fingers to touch the essence of the amazing woman she was.

Ben's whole being was awash with desire. This beautiful, passionate girl was offering herself to him. It seemed she wanted him as much as he wanted her.

He slid the scissors under the lowest loop of her stays and closed the blades. They glanced off the heavy lacing. The corset remained intact. He tried again, snapping the blades together with greater force. The result was the same. He growled in frustration.

Suzanne gave a low chuckle. "Poor Benn." She took the scissors from his hands. "I had forgotten you are left-handed. Unfortunately, my scissors are not." With deft movements, she severed the laces and dropped the scissors back on to the shelf. She was breathing fast now. The corset had been pushed apart by the rise of her bosom and was hanging loosely from its ribbon straps.

Ben swallowed. Then, very slowly, he put his hands to her shoulders and pushed her stays aside. They fell to the floor, landing with a soft thump on the pile of muslin behind her. That left only her chemise. It was so thin that he could see every contour of her body, her erect nipples, her dark navel, the shadow at the junction of her thighs.

He needed more than shadows. In a single swift movement, he seized the hem of her chemise and lifted it. He did not need to ask her to raise her arms. She was before him.

"You are beautiful."

She smiled up into his face, accepting the words that were no more than her due. Then she allowed her gaze to travel slowly over his bare shoulders, over the red silk, still tight around his chest, and down, and down. She lingered over the evidence of his desire. "You are beautiful, too." She moistened her lips with the tip of her tongue and glanced up at him through her lashes. Her eyes were dancing now. She reached for the edge of the silk.

He caught her hand and held it still. "Ah, no, my dear. Not yet. First, it is my turn." He scanned the shelves, pushing aside and then discarding silks and velvets. "Yes. This one, I think." A length of delicate gold silk shimmered as he lifted it down. "You shall be wrapped in gold tissue, as befits a princess."

When she opened her mouth to protest, he silenced her with a short, hard kiss. "Indulge me, I beg of you." He glanced down at the red silk he wore like a badge of honour. "As I have indulged you."

The blush began between her breasts and rose to cover her throat and then her cheeks. For the first time since they had entered the silk store, she seemed shy. But then she raised her chin and nodded.

Ben felt her response, deep in his gut. She would be his. But not yet.

He shook out the fine silk and flung it over Suzanne's shoulders, as she had done to him with the blue velvet. It must not be a cloak, however, for that would hide her beauty. He had something much more revealing in mind. "Raise your arms a little, if you please, lady." A frown flitted across her forehead at his use of her own words, but she did not hesitate. With fingers that seemed to have forgotten their earlier clumsiness, Ben stroked the silk over

73

her shoulders and round her arms before crossing it behind her back. Her arms were pinioned. Her eyes were sparkling.

He brought the free ends round to the front of her body and crossed them again, over her thighs. There was plenty of material left to tuck round behind her calves and under her heels. He stood up to admire what he had done. From the front, her arms and legs were all swathed in gold. A diamond of flesh remained open to his gaze—the narrow base of her throat, her breasts, her swelling hips, the V of her belly narrowing down to the shadow that had tempted him through her chemise. He let his gaze rest there for a moment longer, but desire was overwhelming him. He bent to take one pouting nipple into his mouth, sucking lustily. Suzanne moaned and leaned into him. Ben transferred his mouth to the other, neglected breast. This time she did not moan. She shivered instead.

Ben raised his head and took a step back. "A diamond," he said throatily, drawing the shape in the air. He reached out to brush each glistening nipple with the tip of a finger. "A diamond set with two gleaming rubies." He touched his lips, very lightly, to one nipple and then the other. "A glorious picture in a gilded frame." He bent and bestowed a final kiss on her navel. He would come to the essence of her, and soon, but not until she was ready. He straightened once more and gazed into her eyes. "Would you have me remove these golden trappings? Or should I see whether there are better foils for your beauty here?"

"No," she said softly. "No more." She lifted her heels to free her bonds and shrugged her shoulders. The golden silk whispered across her bare skin and sank reluctantly to the floor. Her arms were free. Her body was naked, proud and ready.

Ben reached for the end of his own red silk.

"No. Let me." Slowly she unwound it from his body, feathering tiny caresses on to his skin as she turned him beneath her hands. When the folded sheet was all that remained, she began to smile, a little. "I do not think this belongs here." With a jerk, she pulled it away from his body and flung it out of the silk store. She sank to her knees and blew a long hot breath over him. "Only the most precious materials have a place here," she said softly. "Only the most beautiful. Which we now have."

Ben did not dare to move. His blood was pounding in his ears. It had to be soon. Without the glorious release of making love, they would both shatter.

It was Suzanne who made the first move. She reached up to pull the pins out of her hair, so that it tumbled down over her shoulders and on to her breast. Very deliberately, she rose from her knees, tossing her head to ensure that her golden curls tickled and teased at his flesh. His reaction was somewhere between a laugh and a groan.

Very satisfying, she decided. There would be no going back now. She put her right hand on his chest, directly over his heart. She could feel its rapid beat. She smiled her message into his eyes. She was willing. She had to make him understand.

A deep breath hissed between his teeth as he knelt to spread the silks on the floor and to make a pillow of her petticoats.

"No!" she cried.

He sprang to his feet. In an instant, his eyes had changed from black to piercing blue. He raised his chin and stared down at her through narrowed eyes. "No? Of course it is no. I promised to protect you, yet I am on the point of robbing you of your honour." His cheeks were slashed with scarlet. His mouth was a hard, uncompromising line. But he made no attempt to cover his proud nakedness.

Suzanne had desired him before. Now her longing was overpowering. This man, the man she loved beyond reason, had allowed her to take him to the brink of fulfilment, yet he was ready to stop at a word. He was doing her honour, not robbing her of it. She gestured towards the silks strewn on the floor. They were her family's future. They must not be damaged.

"Not here." She held out her hand to him, watching as realisation dawned and his gaze mellowed. When he put his fingers into hers, she threw open the door and led him towards the welcoming light of her own bedchamber.

• • • •

Ben tried to lift her into his arms, to carry her across to her bed and lay her between cool sheets. He needed to show her how much he valued her gift.

She shook her head and pushed away his arm. "You are not strong enough yet. You will reopen your wound." She closed the connecting door and turned the key. Then, with graceful strides, she crossed to the main door and locked it also. She was smiling serenely when she turned back to him. For a moment, she leaned her shoulders against the wood, stretching her spine so that her breasts rose invitingly. "No one will disturb us." She crossed to the bed and threw back the covers. The gauzy bedgown slid to the floor, unheeded.

Ben's mouth was dry. He could hardly believe that his wonderful girl, his amazing Suzanne, was offering herself to him. But she was. She was stretched across the bed and beckoning him to join her.

He lay down beside her and pulled her into his arms for a long, passionate kiss. Desire was driving him. He felt no pain at all. His injured shoulder flexed as well as it had ever done. He swept his right hand down her back and cupped her bottom. Then he trailed his fingers delicately up the back of her thigh. She shivered deliciously. He deepened the kiss yet more, glorying in her uninhibited response. She was ready for him. She must be.

He had to be sure. He touched a finger to her inner thigh and let it drift upwards to the core of her. She moaned in response and opened sweetly to his touch. She was more than ready. But, driven though he was, he knew he must go slowly. She was his more than willing partner in this seduction, but it was still her first time. It had to be perfect.

76

He pushed her gently on to her back and nuzzled his way down from her mouth to her breasts, and then to her belly and the tender skin of her inner thighs. The first touch of his tongue at the core of her made her gasp and buck with shock. "Hush, my sweet Suzanne," he crooned, without lifting his head. "Lie still and let me give you pleasure. Feel the waves."

The waves soon became so strong that Suzanne thought she would drown in the wonder of it. Her whole being was focused on that single point, where Benn's tongue was creating such unimagined, piercing pleasure. All at once, it became too much. Her whole body spasmed. She heard herself crying out his name.

A moment later he entered her body, in one long, sustained thrust. She thought she felt a hesitation, but then it was over and he was inside her, fully sheathed. She had wanted this. And it was everything she had desired.

Then he kissed her lips, slowly and sweetly, and began to move. She moaned into his mouth. It felt... She could not describe how it felt. The waves were coming again, washing over her and carrying her even higher than before, as she matched her rhythm to his and strained towards fulfilment. When the climax came, it robbed her of her senses. She saw the bright colours of the rainbow. And then darkness.

• • • •

When she opened her eyes, the light was almost gone. She must have fainted. *No wonder,* she thought, remembering the unbelievable pleasure Benn had given her.

But where was he?

She raised her head from the pillow. He was no longer in her bed. Nor was he anywhere in the room. She sat up with a jerk. It was only then that she saw what he had done. He had covered her naked body with her own bedgown. And then he had left her alone.

What kind of man would do such a thing?

She flung herself out of bed and crossed to the landing door. It was still locked, with the key on the inside. He must have left by the door to the silk store. She would go after him and—

The connecting door was locked and the key was gone. On the floor, in a small neat pile, lay her gown and underthings, folded carefully over the mutilated halves of her corset.

• • • •

Ben could not stop his frenzied pacing. If he stopped moving, his anger and guilt would consume him. What had possessed him to do such a dastardly thing?

He had taken Suzanne's innocence. It did not matter that she had encouraged him to seduce her. The responsibility was his alone. It was hardly surprising if, over the weeks when she had been nursing him, she had come to feel more for him than she ought, for she was a passionate woman. He should have seen the dangers and dealt with them. But he had failed to do so. In the end, the fault was his. He was experienced; she was not. She could not have known what would happen.

He would have to leave soon. What would happen to her then? If anyone discovered what they had done, she would be disgraced, perhaps even cast out of her home. And what if there were to be a child?

He raked his fingers through his hair. It pulled on the roughly healed scar of his head wound, but he ignored it. It would be a judgment on him if it began to bleed again. Suzanne's virgin blood was staining her sheets. What was a little of his own tainted blood by comparison?

He would leave her all the money he had. Yes, that was the answer. It would at least ensure her comfort. She—

No, it was impossible. She would probably throw his money back in his face. And with reason. She had given herself to him in all sweetness. If he offered money, he would be treating her like a whore. She did not deserve that. She deserved to be cherished, by a man who loved and honoured her, a man who would take her to wife. Could Ben find an honest tradesman who would marry her and give her back her standing in *bourgeois* society?

He began to plan. He would need money to buy such a man—ready money now, and the promise of more to follow, once Ben was back in England. But how was Ben to seek out a bridegroom, here in a country that was probably on the brink of war? Ben could not pass for a Frenchman. He could not move around the taverns and coffee houses, bribing the local soaks with drink in hopes of gleaning the information he needed.

Suzanne's husband could not be just anyone. He must be honest and trustworthy. He must be willing to honour Suzanne as his wife, even if she proved to be with child by another man.

A chilling thought shivered through him.

What if this Frenchman were cruel? What if he were to beat her?

Ben saw a vision of Suzanne cowering in the dark in a corner of the silk store, her beautiful face bruised and her limbs trembling in anticipation of beatings still to come. He would not let it happen. He would kill the man first.

Fool. There could be no such man. Suzanne must not be allowed to suffer for Ben's misdeed. A man who loved her would sacrifice everything to protect her.

He stopped in his tracks as the truth of that thought hit him. Like a bolt of lightning, it made every object sharp and clear. It was all very simple. Suzanne had to have a husband who loved her. And Ben had to be that husband. In spite of all his toplofty lectures to himself, in spite of all Jack's warning about falling into parson's mousetrap with a woman who would never be received by Ben's grandfather, Ben had done precisely what he had told himself to avoid. He had fallen in love with his brave and beautiful *bourgeoise.*

He loved her. And he gloried in it.

If she would have him, he would marry her tomorrow. His starchy old grandfather would have to learn to accept her, or lose his grandson altogether. As for the rest of the *ton*, Ben would put a bullet in any man who dared to insult Lord Dexter's wife.

Chapter Twelve

IT WAS WELL AFTER SUPPER time when Ben made his way through the silk store to Suzanne's bedchamber. He had taken great care to put everything to rights. The bolts of silk and velvet had been rewound and restored to the shelves. He could not be absolutely sure that they were all in their assigned places, but he had done his best. This was Suzanne's domain. If anything was amiss, she would put it to rights before anyone else was allowed to set foot inside.

But first he had to restore the keys he had stolen when he left her to wake alone. He had used her own keys to lock her precious silk store against her. He must go to her and beg her pardon. Until that confession was made, he could never offer her his love or his name.

At least this time he was decently clad, in shirt and breeches. Someone—Suzanne?—had washed the blood out of his shirt and carefully mended the torn cloth.

He took one last look round the silk store and put his hand to the door leading to her bedchamber. Earlier, he had locked the connecting door and left the key in the lock on his side. Even if she had a spare, she would not have been able to use it. The door from the silk store to the landing was fastened in the same way. As was the outer door to his own bedchamber. His little fortress was impregnable, until he chose to open the gate.

He tapped gently on the communicating door. There was no answer and no sound from Suzanne's chamber. He breathed a sigh of relief. She was probably still downstairs, seeing to her interminable chores. He would open the door and leave her keys on the dressing table where she was bound to notice them. His confession could wait until later, after she had found them.

He unlocked the door and pushed it open.

She was there.

She was sitting demurely on the end of the bed, fully dressed in a gown made high to the neck, and carefully weaving new laces through the eyelets of her damaged corset.

That damned corset. He felt himself flushing scarlet at the sight of it. It was a symbol of everything he had done, everything that could not be undone. He deserved every single oath he had heaped on himself, and more besides. He was guilty of the worst possible offence—dishonouring the woman he loved. His heart sank to his boots. How could he face her? What could he say?

He saw in an instant that he could not turn back. She was here, and he had to make his confession. He owed it to her. "Suzanne," he said softly. When she did not look up, he said her name again. "Suzanne, I have come to return the keys I took, and to ask your pardon."

She turned to look up at him then. She looked very pale, and quite implacable. "My pardon? For what, may I ask?"

"For everything. I wish to make amends, if you will permit. I took advantage—"

"You took advantage of my good nature to play a silly practical joke in my silk store. I hope you have restored it to order, sir?"

This was going to be even more difficult than Ben had feared. "Suzanne, I need to tell you—"

She silenced him with a proud glare, worthy of a duchess. "I am Miss Grolier to you, sir."

Difficulties, Ben decided on the spot, were invented in order to be overcome. "Miss Grolier, I have put the store to rights as best I can. Will it please you to come and inspect it?" He stood back, holding the door for her.

She sighed. "Very well." She put the corset aside and rose. "We need to resolve matters quickly, I'm sure you will agree. Now that you are recovered, you will wish to be planning your return to England. At the first opportunity." She stalked into the store and began to rearrange the fabrics, tutting crossly as she worked.

Ben stood back, trying not to laugh. She was like a bad-tempered hen, fluffing out its feathers over its brood, turning round and round, but never quite satisfied that everything was exactly as it was meant to be.

She came to the end of the last shelf of fabrics, close by the main door. As she reached out to unlock it, Ben caught her wrist and spun her round to face him. "Your precious silks are safe, my love. But can you forgive me for everything else?"

"There *is* nothing else," she retorted. "Why would I need—?" She broke off and stared at him, her eyes wide. Her body began to sag against the door. Ben had to catch her with his good arm to stop her from falling. "What did you call me?" she asked in a small, shaky voice.

"I called you 'my love' which is, to my mind, a great deal preferable to 'Miss Grolier'. You do agree, I hope?" He gave her no chance to answer. He pulled her hard against his body and began to kiss her as if both their lives depended on it. By the time he was satisfied with her response, they were both gasping for breath and Suzanne's carefully pinned hair had tumbled down on to her shoulders. He lifted one of her curls and began to wind it round his finger. "I take it that is a 'yes', love?"

"I...well, I cannot exactly object to your using such a term of endearment, I suppose. I—"

"You misunderstand me. And wilfully, I do believe." He laughed down into her eyes. "What I need from you, Miss Grolier, *my sweet love,* is your agreement to marry me. As soon as it can be arranged."

"Marry you?" Her voice cracked. "How can I marry you? I don't even know your name."

• • • •

His name, it appeared, really was Ben. He had told her that, but nothing else. They argued, but Ben was adamant. It was too dangerous for her to learn more, he said, while the house was being watched. He might be arrested at any time. Ignorance would help to keep her safe, he maintained stoutly. Besides, what she did not know, she could not betray.

His attitude irked her. Marriage, she responded crisply, was out of the question. She was not about to abandon her home and her family for a nameless English spy, no matter how much he pleaded. Spies, she maintained, were men of the lowest class, even if some of them could *almost* pass for gentlemen.

That comment made Ben laugh a great deal, but he refused to explain why. Instead, he took her in his arms and kissed her until her head was spinning and her bones were beginning to melt. Then he led her back into her bedchamber, sat her down on her bed and left.

She was stunned. What was he thinking? Why had he left her so abruptly?

She listened with the greatest care. There was no scrape of a key turning in the lock. Even without trying the connecting door, she understood that the way to his bed was open to her, if she chose to take it.

He loved her. He wanted to marry her. And he wanted her in his bed. But he was leaving the choices to her. If she went to him, if she lay in his arms, she would never be able to resist him. She loved him. But how could she marry a nameless English spy? How could she abandon all that she was, here in Lyons? She had duties, responsibilities… And her family was in danger, as long as Bonaparte was in France.

Oh, it was impossible. She could not decide. She hesitated, standing by the door. What if—?

The noise was loud enough to penetrate the outside walls plus two communicating doors. What on earth could be happening? Suzanne flung open her door to the silk store at the same time as Ben opened his own.

"Quick. Come and look." He pulled her across to the window, though she noted he did not to allow himself to be seen. There was a great deal of commotion below. All the neighbours seemed to be out in the street. The watcher was back, but now he seemed to be barking orders to a party of soldiers, some carrying flambeaux. They had dragged another silk merchant from his house, three doors away. Some of the onlookers were yelling abuse; some were silent and wary. The merchant's wife stood in the street, wringing her hands and begging for mercy for her man. Her screams and pleas made no difference. In a matter of minutes, he was manacled and led away. The watcher, looking very pleased with himself, followed in the wake of the soldiers.

The locals gazed after them, some still crowing triumphantly, some muttering to each other in low voices and occasionally shaking their heads. A couple of the women led the weeping wife back into her house. The noise subsided. The crowd dispersed. The ugly little tableau was over.

Suzanne felt her shoulders relax a fraction. "Do we dare to hope that our house is no longer in danger?" she asked.

A strong arm stole round her waist. "I think, my love, that we may indeed dare to hope. For many things."

85

Chapter Thirteen

GUILLAUME WAS SO DELIGHTED with the latest developments that he was unusually talkative the following morning when he came upstairs with Ben's hot water. "That old fool further down the street was bound to be arrested. He was much too free with his opinions. Especially after a glass or two. Half of Lyons knew where his sympathies lay."

"Really? When we first saw that spy out there, you all thought he was watching *this* house. All of a sudden, you're remarkably well informed."

The old man grinned. "The way to be well informed, sir, is to frequent certain taverns in this town. Normally I have too many chores to see to in this house, but the mistress said it was vital to the cause. She even gave me silver so that I could buy a drink here and there, where it might help to loosen tongues. It worked, too, though it took hours that I could not really spare. I've had to work twice as hard since, to make up for it."

Ben was not really listening to the man. His thoughts were full of Suzanne. Only Suzanne. *She said we would not be disturbed.* He marvelled at her resourcefulness. A vital spying mission for Guillaume and a quiet house for Suzanne's tryst. Extremely neat. His love was worthy of a place in the Aikenhead Honours. She would make a splendid spy.

Ben decided to voice the question that had started preying on his mind. "Miss Suzanne normally brings up our morning coffee long before this. I hope last night's disturbance has not upset her?"

Guillaume shook his head. "She's sitting in her office, as right as ninepence. I have no doubt she'll be here as soon as she's read her letter."

"What letter?" Ben thundered.

Guillaume did not know the identity of the sender. All he could say was that the handwriting was not Marguerite's.

Ben hastily wiped off the last of the shaving soap. The letter might bring vital intelligence. He must risk going downstairs, even though he might be seen.

As he reached the hallway, Suzanne came flying out into the hall. "Oh, Ben, I have such wonderful news. Marguerite and Jacques are married." She waved her letter. "I don't understand it all, but that part is beyond doubt. Jacques has taken Marguerite to his family in England."

Ben twitched the letter out of her fingers and began to read. It was from the curé in Normandy, who wrote in a cryptic style much like Marguerite's. Her elder sister had married her betrothed, the letter said. Did that mean Jack? Ben supposed it must do. There was a paragraph of pious advice to Suzanne about never allowing her heart to rule her head. That was wise, but a little late now.

The final paragraph was very puzzling. Ben pulled Suzanne into her office and closed the door firmly. Then he scanned that paragraph again. "What on earth does it mean? How can your mama's assessment of Marguerite's betrothed have been exactly right? And why should that make him a most suitable husband?"

"I'm sorry, I'm afraid I don't understand that, either. Perhaps I should ask mama? She will have to be told about Marguerite's marriage, in any case. She will be cross, I dare say, that Jacques did not ask her permission."

"From Normandy?"

"It is the way things have always been done in our family. Mama thinks she is still entitled to the privileges of rank, even though we—" She stopped short and let out a long, shuddering breath. Her eyes grew round. "I remember now. What mama said. About Jack. But surely not—? And yet, it must have been that. It was the only time she saw them together."

Ben threw the letter onto the desk and took her by the shoulders, as if he were about to shake her. "Suzanne, what on *earth* are you talking about? You make no sense at all."

She smiled beatifically. "Tell me, Ben," she began innocently, "was mama right when she said that your Jack is the son of a duke?"

"Oh, lor—"

"Well, *is* he?"

"Er...yes. But a younger son only." He grinned down at her. "He's number three, actually. There is no chance that your sister will end up a duchess, I'm afraid."

Suzanne made a fist and punched his arm. His good arm, Ben noticed. Even angry, she was not risking damage to his wounded shoulder.

"That was not what I was asking, and you know it perfectly well. This Jack of yours. Exactly who is he?"

"The younger son of a duke," he said unhelpfully.

She growled, deep in her throat. She sounded like an angry kitten and he longed to stroke her into a purr. He even started to run his fingers down her arm, but she shook him off. "You are avoiding the question, Ben. Are you refusing to tell me the identity of the man who has married my own sister?"

"Yes. It is safer so."

"Why, you—" She made to strike him again. Much harder this time.

"No, love," he said gently, catching her wrist and pulling her hard against his body. He wrapped his arms round her protectively. "Believe me, it *is* safer so. For, eventually, I will have to leave you here, without a protector, apart from Guillaume. If you do not know Jack's real identity, you can lay your hand on the bible and swear that you never learned his name. It is not much, but it may help to keep you safe. It is all I can do."

"But you will take me with you, will you not? Jack took Marguerite."

"Marguerite will be safe in England by now. So there is no danger in her learning who Jack is. But here… Suzanne, my dearest heart, I will take you with me if you truly wish it, but have you considered…? Jack's orders were for me to make my way out through Spain, to take ship from there. It will be a hard journey, through the mountains. I would not subject you to that. I—"

"Pooh. I am not such a weakling."

"You have a core of steel, my love. I know that. But you have a dutiful heart, too. What if Guillaume is taken, forced to enlist? They are conscripting married men now, since Bonaparte ordered the mobilisation. They may soon take old men, too. And what of your mama? Can you truly leave her alone here? Forgive me, but we could not take her with us. Such a journey would be impossible with her. Surely you must see that?"

"Oh. Oh dear." She crumpled a little in his arms. "If I left with you, I would be abandoning my family to…to…I do not know what possible fate. And who would run the business? Who would put food on the table? Guillaume cannot do so alone, even if he is spared enlistment. Besides, mama would pay no heed to him and who knows what she might do? When she takes one of her strange fancies into her head, it sometimes takes all three of us—Berthe and Guillaume and me—to pacify her."

She swallowed hard. "You are right, Ben. You must leave. As long as Bonaparte is on the loose, your duty calls you back to England. And I…I must do my duty here. I will stay to look after mama."

He kissed her then. It began as a kiss of consolation, gentle and loving, but desire soon ignited in both of them and, within seconds, they were kissing passionately, unable to get enough of each other. He cupped her breast and began to push aside her bodice. He needed to touch her delicate skin.

She groaned and pushed away from him. They were both flushed and breathing hard. "Not here," she said with a tiny smile. She glanced towards the office door. She was right. Anyone might walk in on them. Had he been out of his mind?

"Forgive me, love," he said, and meant it. He saw all too clearly what he had to do. And it hurt.

Her smile widened. "You shall have everything you want. Tonight. In my chamber, upstairs."

Ben held her gaze and slowly—very slowly—shook his head. "No."

Her smile died on her lips. The sparkle left her glorious eyes.

"No," he said again, "there will be no more…er…dalliance outside of wedlock. I intend to marry you, Suzanne Grolier, and my honour requires me to master my passions until I have done so."

"And when will your precious honour allow that to be?" she asked coldly.

"As soon as I return for you, naturally. Bonaparte will be defeated—Wellington will see to that, I am certain—but it may take some months. In the meantime, you will remain here, with your mama, and you will be simply a hardworking silk-weaver, with no interest at all in who governs France. If you keep the household out of politics, you will be safe until I can return."

Suzanne could not say a word. His *honour*, indeed. How could he be so pompous? And so thoughtless? Had it not occurred to him that she might already be with child? She would certainly not be safe in Lyons if she were seen to be an unmarried girl with a big belly.

Something must have shown in her face, for he said, anxiously, "What is it, love? What are you afraid of? Tell me."

She had no choice. "What if I am already with child, Ben?" she whispered. "What then?"

His face turned ashen. And there was real fear in his eyes. Not for himself, she was sure, but for her.

• • • •

"We will be married here, *now*, before I leave for England," Ben declared, trying to make his voice sound firm and decisive. Fear was knotting his gut at the thought of the danger Suzanne might be in, left alone in Lyons, with no strong arm to protect her. If she were seen to be pregnant, and unmarried, she would be cried a whore. And in these uncertain times, the local people might easily turn against her. What if that ugly crowd down in the street were to—?

"And precisely *how* would such a marriage protect me?" she demanded angrily, taking another step back from him and wrapping her arms around herself. "I cannot declare myself married to an Englishman, or even to the German you were pretending to be, for both are enemies now. All Europe is allied against us. They say another invasion will begin any day now. Even royalists are joining the militia to defend France." She swallowed a sound in her throat that could have been a sob. Of anger? Or of fear? Then she shook her head so vehemently that her curls began to dance around her face, highlighting how pale she had become. "Probably better to be with child by an unknown lover than to be married to the enemy."

It was as if she had struck him. Ben could neither move or speak. He stared at her. She had said she loved him, but now she was throwing his proposal back in his face. And calling him "the enemy".

Suzanne glared back at him. She was now so pale that her skin seemed tinged with grey. Finally, she blinked rapidly and ran for the door.

"Suzanne, wait."

Too late. She was gone.

Ben clawed desperately at the tangle of thoughts and feelings rioting through his brain. She had rejected him. Perhaps she did not really love him? But she might be carrying his child. How was he to protect her if she would not marry him?

He put his good hand to his forehead and thumped hard. *Think.* He needed to think. Logically. Feelings were too dangerous here. What he needed was a careful plan. He needed to assess all the risks and find a way of defeating them, one by one.

He forced himself to take long deep breaths. Yes, he must make a plan.

A heavy cart rumbled past in the street outside. Good grief, he was still standing downstairs in Suzanne's office, where anyone might spy him by peering through the window. His wits had clearly gone a-begging.

He ran for the door. He did at least have the presence of mind to check that the hall was empty before venturing out and making for the stairs. Moments later, he had regained the relative safety of his bedchamber.

He glanced across at the door to the silk store, wondering if Suzanne was in her bedchamber on the far side. Poor darling. She had been so distressed. She had been on the point of tears when she fled from the office. He should go through to her and—

No. He should not. First, he had to have a decent plan. Suzanne was in real danger and warm words would not be enough. She would reject him again and—now that he was beginning to think clearly once more—he could understand why. Perhaps he should take her with him through Spain after all? Perhaps it would be possible to hire good people here in Lyons to help look after her mama? Surely Suzanne would know someone who could be trusted?

He shook his head despairingly. Far more questions than answers. This would not do. He had to start again from the beginning.

He took another deep breath and began to pace.

Chapter Fourteen

SUZANNE WAS SHIVERING, HORRIFIED at what she had done. She had accused Ben—the man she loved beyond family, beyond country, beyond reason—of being the enemy. What on earth had possessed her?

Fear.

Her deepest, darkest fears had been driving her. And they still did.

She let herself sink down onto her bed. She had to. Her legs were so wobbly they would barely hold her weight.

She knew what the Lyons mob could do to fallen women. She had seen such women stripped to their shifts and dragged out by the hair. Whipped as whores. And worse. No punishment for the guilty men, naturally. That scene out in the street with the poor blabbermouth silk-merchant had been mild by comparison with some of the beatings Suzanne had witnessed over the years. And the rumours of another invasion had all the local men spoiling for a fight. Everyone was jumpy and ready with fists and knives. She had seen that before, too.

Marriage to Ben—not that it was possible—would probably put her in even more danger. Instead of being whipped at the cart tail, she might well be executed as a traitor to France. That neighbour had been carted off to prison for saying the wrong things, not for actually doing anything in support of the royalist cause. Whereas Suzanne had given shelter to two English spies. And now she was seriously thinking about marrying one of them?

If she was lucky, Bonaparte's men would simply shoot her.

The mental image of herself standing in front of a firing squad was so clear, and so ridiculously melodramatic, that she began to laugh and laugh. Soon, tears were pouring down her cheeks. Was she losing her mind?

She was so very much alone. If Marguerite had been here, things would have been different. The sisters had always been close. They had shared everything. But Marguerite was gone to England, married now to her son of a duke. So there was no one left in whom Suzanne could confide. Since the accident, mama lived mostly in a fantasy world of her own. Old Berthe was intensely loyal, but her main concern was for making mama's strange half-life as comfortable as possible. And though Guillaume loved both Grolier sisters as if they were his own daughters, he would be outraged if he learned what Suzanne and Ben had done.

No, for Suzanne there was no one.

Suzanne sighed deeply and wiped away her tears. Strangely, her mad outburst had made her feel slightly better. She could see more clearly now. She had to go forward from where she was. And she would. Not everything was to be feared. She had sinned, but she had done good deeds, too. She had saved Ben and helped to save Jack. She had been loyal to her family's cause. She had taken charge of the household and proved that she could run the business alone. Marguerite would be proud of her. And now Suzanne would continue to discharge her duty to her mama and the rest of the household. What else was there? Dwelling on past mistakes was torture and achieved nothing. The past could not be undone.

Besides, she might not be pregnant after all.

• • • •

Ben deliberately rattled the lock as he turned the key in the door between the silk store and Suzanne's bedchamber. She needed to know he was there. She needed to agree to speak to him. He would not go a step further unless she invited him in.

He rapped on the wood and waited.

Nothing.

He rapped again, louder this time. Still no response. And yet he was sure she was there, on the far side of the door. Was she too angry, or too consumed by her fears, to let him show his face?

"Suzanne. Please let me in, my love. We need to talk. Please, Suzanne. I have plans for keeping you safe. I need to tell you what they are."

A swift step and the door was thrown open, flooding the dark store with light. For a second, Ben was dazzled. All he could see was the light streaming through her fair curls, making a halo around her shadowed features as she confronted him.

"*Your* plans, sir? What gives you the right to tell me what to do?"

Ben gritted his teeth and swore silently. He was making a complete mull of this, and it mattered more than anything he had ever done before. He must not make another mistake. If he did, he could lose her.

He did not cross the threshold into her domain. He stood where he was, waiting for his eyes to adjust to the light. When they did, he saw that she was distressed and that she had been weeping. But there were no tears now; her eyes were sparking fury at him. Angry red patches were starting to bloom, high on her pale cheeks.

"Forgive my clumsy words, love," he began. "I have no rights over you. I know that. But I love you with all my heart and...and I worry about what might happen to you. Might I...might we talk? About what we could do to keep you safe? Together?"

She took a step back and gestured for him to enter her chamber.

Progress, though her expression remained grim.

Ben marched straight across to the far side of the room and leant his back against the wall by the window. He was putting himself as far from Suzanne as it was possible to be in that small chamber. If he was to remain rational, there had to be space between them. He did not dare to touch her.

Suzanne watched him for a moment with narrowed eyes. Then she gave a little nod and sat down on the far edge of her bed, half-turned away from him. He could not see her eyes. He could barely see one side of her face. But at least the spots of anger seemed to be fading.

There was hope. Provided he was careful.

"I...I was wrong to assume that marriage would solve everything. I see that now. But I am not your enemy, Suzanne. I could never be your enemy. I love you."

She sighed and bent her head over her clasped hands. "Yes, I know that," she said at last, in a tiny voice. "But it changes nothing. And, in any case, marriage is impossible for us. There is not a single priest in the neighbourhood who could be trusted with the secret of who we—who you are."

With all his pacing, he had not thought of that. He groaned. She was right. He had been so determined not to put her in even greater danger by revealing his identity. But, to marry her, he would need to give his real name and station to a priest and, presumably, to write it in a register for all to see. That was worse than clumsy; it was monumentally stupid.

He swallowed hard and tried a different tack. "How soon will you know if we—if you are...er...increasing?"

Her blush was deep and instant. It even reached the back of her neck and rose into her hairline. He thought she gave a tiny mew of pain.

Clumsy, and crass to boot. Could he possibly have said anything worse? And what could he say now? How was he to reach her?

Before he could say another word, she turned her back on him completely. Clearly, she could not bear to face him at all. When she spoke, she seemed to be addressing the wall of the silk store. "Not long. Two or three weeks at most. I..." The back of her neck reddened even more. "I have never been... I cannot exactly predict..." She ran out of words. No wonder, considering how deeply he had embarrassed her.

The answer came to him in that instant. Yes, it was his duty to return to England, but why so soon? Why now? The extra information he had gleaned would almost certainly be useless by the time he had struggled through the Spanish mountains and found a ship for home. Bonaparte was mobilising a huge army. Wellington would learn of that and be making plans to counter it, long before Ben reached even the French border with Spain. The intelligence that really mattered had gone with Jack, and he had already reached England.

"Suzanne, I will—" He stopped short. That would not do. He began again. "If you permit, my love, I will stay here with you in Lyons until you...er...know. One way or the other."

She spun round. Her eyes were huge in her pale face. "What? But you cannot. You will be in danger if you stay in Lyons."

She was worrying about *him*.

He wanted to move towards her, to take her in his arms. Oh, she was a jewel of a girl and he—

He stopped himself just in time and forced his weight back against the wall. Luckily, Suzanne's eyes had been on his face. It seemed she had not noticed his tiny shift towards her. If she had, and if she had come to him, he would have lost all ability to think rationally. He had to stay in control here. Of himself.

She was worrying about him. So she did love him. So he *had* to defend her. Eventually, he would find a safe way of giving her the protection of his name. Until then, he would protect her with his body. And with his life, if necessary.

A sharp and all-too-rational voice echoed in his head. *Fool. If you give your life for her before you have given her your name, you will condemn her, twice over.*

He decided, on the spot, that he would not leave her side until they were safely married. "I am in danger here and I am in danger travelling to Spain. What matters, love, is to keep *you* out of danger." He would find a way to marry her, somehow. He had to. He might be killed en route to Spain; he might be wrecked in a storm and die at sea. As his widow, and possibly the mother of his child, Suzanne would have a position of honour and a claim on his estate; as his unmarried lover, she would have worse than nothing at all. He could not risk that for her.

But he could not tell her so now. If he did, she would rail at him, tell him it was impossible, insist that he flee. Alone.

He smiled, confidently, he hoped. "If you will permit," he said again, "I will remain in hiding here until we…er…know. Then I will make my way to Spain. I had thought that perhaps you might come with me?"

"But mama…? You know I cannot. My duty is here."

"Would it not be possible," he began gently, "to hire someone to look after your mama? Is there no one in Lyons whom you can trust? I have gold. I can pay." And in friendly Spain, it would be safe to find a priest to marry them. If Ben had his way, they would be wed as soon as they crossed the border.

Suzanne shook her head, a little sadly. "There is no one. Only Berthe and Guillaume, who have served our family since we—since before I was born. They are devoted to mama and they know all about the accident that caused her to be…to be as she is. Sometimes she can be violent, screaming and raging. Sometimes she seems perfectly rational but then, a moment later, she has weird fancies and says strange things. Royalist things. An outsider might repeat them to others. And if they were believed, who knows what Bonaparte's agents might do?"

Ben's heart sank. Unfortunately, what she said about Madame Grolier was true. There had been several violent scenes in the house these last few weeks. And Ben could not forget Jack's account of how the haughty dame had forced him to swear an oath on the family bible. She had behaved, Jack said, like an old-fashioned French aristocrat rather than the wife of a *bourgeois* silk-weaver. Bonaparte's agents might make a great deal of something like that. And if they came to search the house, what might they find, even if Ben was already gone? A fervently royalist household was bound to have some incriminating material somewhere.

"I understand. And I will not press you to come with me to England, I promise. Not until it is safe to bring your mama and the servants as well. But, please, Suzanne, please let me stay for these next few weeks. I will do nothing to put your household in danger. I will sit up here and clean boots if you want me to. If you will only let me stay."

She gazed at him for a long time. Then, with a fleeting frown and a little shake of her head, she rose and crossed to the door to the silk store. Retrieving the key from the inside, she held the door open for him. "Very well," she said quietly, "you may stay. I will tell Guillaume that you are not yet well enough to travel and need a week or two more to regain your strength. You will remain hidden in your chamber. Guillaume will bring you chores to do, to keep you occupied. And whenever he sees you, you will make sure you appear suitably weak, but improving. Slowly."

Ben made to speak, but Suzanne had not finished. "As for this door, it will remain locked. From my side."

Ben was so relieved he almost laughed. But that would certainly have offended his prickly love, so he forced himself to give her a submissive smile instead. "I am at your service, ma'am." He walked slowly across the floor and through the door she was holding. As he crossed the threshold into the dark delights of the silk store, he could not resist adding wickedly, "In all things."

She slammed the door at his back. And turned the key in the lock before he could say another word.

Chapter Fifteen

SUZANNE WAS TRYING TO KEEP her mind on her weaving. The shuttle moved steadily to and fro, to and fro, to and fro. She tried to focus on the flow of the silk thread through the warp, and the regular movement of her feet on the pedals, but it was monotonous work. Her body could do it by itself, leaving her mind free to wander. And to misbehave.

More than two weeks of waiting, and worrying, had not helped her peace of mind. Nor had her stubborn determination to stay out of Ben's bed. She had visited him, very occasionally, in his bedchamber but she had always made sure that she was accompanied by one of the servants. Such visits, she told herself, were necessary to ensure that their hidden spy was truly mending and was posing no threat to their vulnerable little household. On one such visit, she had even lectured Ben sternly about the need to keep well away from the window. She reminded him that there were always Bonapartist sympathisers in the street below and that, if Ben were spotted, disaster for the Groliers could follow.

Ben had responded meekly, promising to do everything she asked, but avoiding her eye. Old Berthe might have been taken in, but Suzanne knew he was nothing like as calm as he appeared. She didn't even have to look at him; she could sense the emotions hidden behind his bland mask. He was at least as worried as she was. In fact, it was worse for him in some ways, since he was effectively imprisoned in one single room. No wonder he was feeling impotent.

Impotence led to frustration. What if Ben decided to do something drastic?

Not for the first time, Suzanne tried to persuade herself that she was fretting over nothing. Ben could not leave the house without help. Not unless he decided to walk to Spain. If he sent the kitchen boy to fetch a horse, Suzanne would learn of it. The kitchen boy was simple, but she had made very sure he understood that he would lose his place if he obeyed instructions from anyone but Suzanne without warning her first. No amount of silver from Ben would make up for the risk of being thrown out into the street to starve. Even a simpleton could understand that.

There was no risk that Guillaume or Berthe would help Ben, either. Guillaume wanted Ben out of the house, certainly, for he had serious misgivings about Ben's intentions towards Suzanne. Protestations of love and future marriage were not to be trusted, he said, not from an Englishman. Guillaume would not even accept a marriage before a priest, unless he witnessed it with his own eyes. Guillaume was a royalist, and totally loyal to the Grolier family, but England was "Perfidious Albion", as he had reminded Suzanne more than once. Treachery was England's traditional response, whenever it suited her purposes. And English men were no different.

Ben would never betray me. He loves me. He does. Why else would he be risking his life to remain here, waiting, until I know whether... No, if he did not love me, he would have left us, long ago.

The thread caught and broke.

Suzanne swore aloud, then clapped her hand over her mouth and glanced round to check if she had been overheard. What on earth was happening to her? She had been brought up to behave better than that. Luckily, she was still alone in the weaving room. No one had heard her outburst.

Mechanically, she set about repairing the break and ensuring there would be no flaw in the finished silk. It was not a difficult task for someone as skilled as Suzanne. But she knew that, if she had been paying proper attention to her work instead of daydreaming, the break would not have happened in the first place.

There. It's done. And for the rest of the day, I will take more care.

The shuttle began its monotonous journey again. To and fro, to and fro, to and—

"Argh!" The pain was so sharp that Suzanne dropped the shuttle and doubled up over the loom. She put both hands to her belly and pressed hard, groaning all the while. Stomach cramps were often a problem at the start of her courses, but they were not usually as bad as this. She bit her lip to stop herself from crying out again.

Was this the start of her courses? Or something else?

Whichever it is, I am not carrying Ben's child.

Her mind was numb. All her feelings seemed to have been frozen into nothingness by that single, terrible spasm of pain. It was utterly final. There would be no child.

No child.

She rose from her seat and put her hands to the small of her back, trying to force herself to stand straight in spite of the pain.

The daughter of the Marquise de Jerbeaux did not stoop, no matter what the circumstances. She had been taught that from the cradle.

She raised her chin and made for the door. There were practical things to be done. She would go to her chamber for the cloths to deal with her courses. Then she would go to the kitchen to make a tisane to ease the cramps. That usually worked within an hour or so; she should be able to come back to her weaving quite quickly. This silk needed to be finished soon and she was behind with her work. She was in charge of the Grolier silk business, after all, and—

I have to tell him.

But how *do I tell him? What do I say?*

Would he be sorry? Or would he be glad? It was impossible to predict his reaction.

Even if he had wanted the child, he would never admit it to her. He would be bound to concentrate on the fact that Suzanne was much, much safer here in France if she was not increasing.

He had said he would stay until they knew. Once she told him, he could leave for Spain, and England.

She did not want him to leave.

The longer he stayed, the greater the danger to him, and to the whole household. The safest solution, for all of them, was for Ben to leave.

The spasm of pain hit again and this time Suzanne crumpled to the floor and lay there, curled like a babe, weeping silently for the loss she could not understand.

• • • •

Suzanne did not visit Ben's room for two whole days. She blamed it on her stomach cramps, which were much worse than usual and made her weak and weepy. She promised herself she would visit him—and tell him—as soon as she was stronger.

On the third day, she still could not face him. She spent her time in the weaving room, instead.

"Mistress, may I speak to you? In private?" Guillaume was looking stern, but also a little furtive.

Suzanne looked round the room. The doors and windows were closed. No one could hear them. She rose from her loom and went to him. "Certainly," she said calmly, though her pulse was rioting. What was the matter? Had Ben—?

Guillaume lowered his voice even further. "Mistress, our visitor is perfectly recovered now. I caught him doing exercises in his chamber and there's clearly nothing wrong with him at all. I suspect he has an ulterior motive for wishing to remain. I think he has designs on you. I do not trust him and you should not do so, either. 'Perfidious Albion', remember? You need to tell him to leave. As soon as may be."

"But how can he possibly leave? He will need a horse and Bonaparte has requisitioned all the available animals, has he not?" Men, horses and equipment had been leaving Lyons on a daily basis, heading for the northern army or for the defensive positions on the eastern frontier.

Guillaume ignored her question and shook his head sorrowfully. "You are not surprised to learn that he is well enough to leave, are you? How long have you known? It is not my place to judge you, mistress, but I have loved you since the cradle and... Mistress, I beg you, do not allow yourself to be deceived by this man. He will ruin you. And then he will abandon you."

Suzanne drew herself up very straight. "He will not," she spat. "He will return once Bonaparte is defeated and then we will be married. His friend Jack married Marguerite. You know he did. Why should not Ben do the same for me?"

"Mr Jacques swore a sacred oath on the bible. In front of your mama. He had no choice if he was not to lose all honour. Your Herr Benn has sworn no oath. Private promises to a green girl are easily broken."

The words were barely out of his mouth when his "green girl" slapped him so hard that his head was knocked sideways.

"Mistress," he gasped, shocked.

Suzanne felt the colour flooding into her face. She must be quite as red as the hand print on Guillaume's cheek. But she would not apologise. He was wrong, wrong, wrong. He must be. Ben was an honourable man. And he loved Suzanne.

She turned for the door. Without looking back at Guillaume, she threw angry words over her shoulder, "I am going upstairs to speak to Herr Benn. Alone. I shall decide for myself whether he is well enough to leave for Spain. And, in the meantime, you had better start making discreet enquiries about transport. However much you want rid of him, you will never succeed if you don't find him a horse."

Chapter Sixteen

SUZANNE RACED UP THE STAIRS to the door of Ben's bedchamber. There, she stopped dead, her fury overtaken by uncertainty. She had no idea what to say to him. She only knew that she had to find a way of telling him there would be no child. And she had to encourage him to leave, for all their sakes. Her stomach pains gripped even more fiercely at the prospect of the encounter ahead of her.

Since when have I been such a coward? I have to face him. Now. And if he really loves me, he will help me through this.

Before she could lose what little courage remained to her, she rapped loudly on Ben's door.

She expected him to bid her enter, but he did not. Instead she heard quick, booted steps on the floorboards and then the door was thrown wide.

"I told you that—" His jaw dropped and his eyes widened. "Suzanne. Forgive me, I was expecting Guillaume and I—" He peered past her into the dark landing. "You are alone? No chaperon today? I am honoured." He stood back and made a sweeping gesture. "Pray enter, ma'am. I am at your service, as ever."

He was treating her like a queen, so she would behave like one. She straightened her back, lifted her chin, and sailed into his chamber.

Behind her, he closed the door very quietly. He neither moved nor spoke. He was waiting for her to begin.

Suzanne took a long, deep breath and turned. The man she loved was leaning casually against the closed door, one booted foot crossed over the other. As she watched, he raised his left hand and stroked his jaw like an absent-minded academic, but Suzanne could see that his pose was nothing but a fraud, for there was clear tension in the corded muscles of his neck and in his narrowed gaze, fixed on her face.

He was worried, and anxious. Because he loved her.

She felt the beginnings of a flush of heat in her face but she forced herself to keep looking straight at him. She loved him. And he loved her. Between true lovers, there should be no secrets, and no embarrassment, surely?

Her words began tumbling out in a rush. "I have come to tell you that I— That I have begun my—" Oh, it was all coming out wrong. She put both hands to her flaming cheeks and made herself continue. "Ben, I have to tell you that there will not be a...a child. What we did together— That is, I am not—"

Before she could finish, he had crossed the floor and pulled her into his arms. It was an embrace of comfort, not of passion. He did not even attempt to kiss her. He simply held her close against his warmth and strength, stroking her hair and making gentling noises, as if he were soothing a frightened child.

"Oh, Ben, I..." Her words ended on a sob, though she did not know why. She was so confused. She buried her face in his shirt so that he would not see her tears. She could not bear that he would think her weak.

"Hush, love, hush." He dropped a kiss on her hair and continued his hypnotic stroking. "I am sure you are feeling unwell but, please, try to dry your tears. It is for the best, however much we might both regret that you are not with child. What matters is that you will be safe now. We must hold to that and be glad. Once we are married, and living together in England, we will have all the time in the world for the gift of children." He dropped another gentle kiss on

109

her hair. "And believe me, sweetheart, there will be much joy in the getting of them."

The hint of mischief in his final words made her swallow her tears and chuckle, half in embarrassment, half in wonder. She snuggled further into his warmth and slid her arms round his back. "You are a wicked man," she murmured softly against the fine lawn of his shirt.

"But you love me, in spite of my wickedness, do you not?"

She raised her head to look into his eyes. They were indeed sparkling with mischief but, behind the twinkle, there was something much deeper. Suzanne was not sure that Ben would ever be able to put his emotions into words, but for her it did not matter. She knew what he felt for her. His love was deep, and true, and for ever.

As was hers.

"I love you, for *everything* you are, and I always will," she said, meaning every word.

"Mmm." His gaze softened and he bent to drop a tiny kiss on her lips. But he pulled away almost instantly, before she could begin to kiss him back. "No more, love, for you know where kisses lead." He smiled ruefully. "What matters is to keep you safe." He put her from him and then raised her right hand to his lips. "Chaste kisses on the fingertips. Nothing more. Not until we are wed, and I can get you safe to England."

The touch of his lips shivered up her fingers. England. Where there was safety for Ben. And the fulfilment of duty.

"You will leave for England," she said flatly, trying to ensure there was no hint of doubt in her tone. "The militias are gathering to defend France. There will be blood on the streets, even if Wellington wins the great battle. Scores will be settled. I have seen it before. You must leave for Spain now, while there is still time."

"But you will be in danger…"

She shook her head. "We will be safe enough. We have weathered this before. We are weavers, plying our trade and selling our wares to anyone who can pay. As far as the outside world is concerned, House Grolier has no politics. Our walls are strong. If there is unrest in the streets, we will bar the doors and windows and wait until it is over. We have done that before, too," she finished with a decisive nod. She did not add that, on previous occasions, she had had her older sister by her side to take the lead.

Ben frowned for a moment. Then he sighed out a long breath and Suzanne saw that she had won. *It is for the best*, she told herself. *It is the only way to keep him safe. He has to go.*

"You know your own business best. I have to accept that, though I—" He sighed again and drove a hand through his hair. It made him look very young. And vulnerable. "But I would need transport. Are there coaches still running to Marseilles? It would take much too long to walk all the way to Spain."

Suzanne shook her head. "Everything is in turmoil. Bonaparte has requisitioned the horses from all the livery stables and posting inns for the army. And, in any case, all the men are so busy in the defence forces that no one is going anywhere by coach or chaise. I have asked Guillaume to try to find you a horse from somewhere else. It will probably cost some of that gold of yours, though."

Ben made a face. "That will have to do. But it will be plaguey slow going if I cannot change horses on the road."

That was true. And the slower Ben travelled, the greater the risk of his being captured by the Bonapartists and shot as a spy.

"Perhaps we could find you two riding horses?" Suzanne ventured hopefully. "That way, you would have a fresh mount of your own. Would that not help?"

"Well... Yes, I suppose it might." Ben's mind was racing, but on another tack altogether. If he had two horses, he could take Suzanne with him to Spain and marry her there. She would insist on returning to Lyons, to take care of her mama, but at least she would have the protection of his name.

And who would protect her on the trip back to Lyons?

She could not ride back alone, and Ben could not return with her. As a plan, it was hopeless.

Suzanne cocked an ear towards the window. "That's odd. I'm sure I heard a horse then. In the street outside the house. If Guillaume has found you a horse already, I shall kiss him." She motioned to Ben to stay where he was, while she went to the window. She pushed herself up on tiptoe so that she could see as much of the street below as possible. She strained forward, leaning both hands on the sill. Then she gasped and began to giggle. "Oh, dear. Oh, Ben, I am sorry to have given you false hopes. I did hear hooves on the cobbles, but it is not a horse." She giggled again and held up a warning hand. "No, don't come to look. You really must not be seen. They do look funny, though. Our hooved friend down below is a tiny little donkey, with a very fat priest on his back. It's astonishing that the poor animal can move at all with such a burden."

"Donkeys are pretty strong. Or perhaps it is a mule?"

Suzanne seemed not to hear Ben's question, but she did turn to look at him. "I wonder what that priest is doing here in our street," she mused. "I don't think I have ever seen him before." She shook her head sadly. "All strangers are dangerous nowadays. Even priests can be spies."

That was no doubt why she would not trust any of the local priests to marry them. And why there was no way out of Ben's dilemma. He had promised himself not to leave her until they were safely married, but there could be no safe marriage here in France.

The sound of rushing feet on the stairs was followed by a hurried knock on the bedchamber door. Half a second later, Guillaume charged in. "Mistress, you must come downstairs at once," he gasped.

How dare he make such a demand? They were doing nothing improper, for Suzanne was still by the window while Ben was standing in the shadows, several feet from her. Ben was not about to put up with impertinence from a servant, however venerable. "I did not give you leave to enter my room," he snarled.

Guillaume totally ignored him. The old man rushed across to Suzanne, grabbed her by the arm and began to pull her towards the door. "Mistress, you must come at once," he said again.

Suzanne resisted. "What on earth is the matter with you, Guillaume? I thought I sent you out to find a horse."

"I have found something much better," Guillaume announced proudly. "Father Bertrand is here."

• • • •

In the end, it was safer to bring Father Bertrand up to Ben's bedchamber than for Ben to go downstairs to meet him.

From Suzanne's description of the overburdened donkey, Ben had expected to meet a large man, but the curé who came panting up the stairs was very short, though very round. When the priest removed his wide-brimmed hat, Ben saw that the little man was also almost completely bald. But his round face was beaming, even as he gasped for breath.

"Suzanne!" he exclaimed from the doorway, making the sign of the cross in her direction. "My dear child, how wonderful to see you again after all these years."

"Father Bertrand. It *is* you. But Marguerite wrote that you were in Rouen. I don't understand. How do you come to be here in Lyons? Especially now."

"It is a long story, my dear, and I... Might I sit down? I have been travelling since first light and my old bones are weary." He took a few unsteady steps into the room.

Ben pushed a chair forward and bowed to the little man.

Guillaume was still hovering in the doorway. "Shall I bring up some wine, mistress? And some food for monsieur le curé?"

"Yes, if you—" she began.

"That would be kind, but see to my poor beast first, if you would, Guillaume. His needs are much greater than mine." The curé dropped his hat on to the floor and sank gratefully into the chair. He let out a long gusty sigh. "Thank you, my son."

Ben bowed again and waited to see what would happen next. From what Suzanne had said, Ben supposed that this must be the curé who had married Jack and Marguerite, and who had helped them to escape to England. So this priest could be trusted. Couldn't he?

"Marguerite told me about *madame*, your mother. About the accident. I would have come before, Suzanne, if only I had known. Your poor papa, too. He was a good man." The little man crossed himself again and shook his head sadly. "Such a tragedy to lose him when you have already borne so much."

Ben swallowed a gasp. Suzanne's father was dead? She had lied to him.

"May I see *madame*? Do you think she will remember me?" the curé asked gently.

Suzanne was paying no attention to Ben. She sank to her knees by the priest's chair and gazed up at him. "I do not know, Father. She has good days and bad days. But...but she is gradually getting worse. It is dangerous for Berthe to leave her alone. She has more and more bad days." She swallowed a sob. "Her mind is going. We are losing her."

Ben was beginning to feel truly guilty now, at the sight of Suzanne's distress. Both her parents were lost to her. The whole family was vulnerable. The Grolier sisters had probably lied to the whole world, in an effort to protect those they loved. It was brave. It was admirable.

The priest laid a gentle hand on Suzanne's head. "Do not weep, my child. I have come to give you what help I may. Now, will you have the goodness to introduce your...er...friend?"

114

Chapter Seventeen

SUZANNE BLUSHED AND ROSE to her feet, reaching for Ben's hand to draw him forward. "I beg your pardon, Father. This is Ben. He was calling himself Herr Christian Benn when he first arrived, but now it is just...just Ben."

The curé smiled up at Ben. "Forgive me if I do not rise, sir, but I am honoured to meet you at last. Lord Jack told me what had happened to you in Marseilles. How goes it with your wound? Are you fully recovered?"

Although it was clear that the little priest knew a great deal about Jack and about the Grolier family, Ben was still wary. "Forgive me, Father, but exactly what did Jack tell you about us?"

"Well," the curé began, "not very much at first. But once the pair of them had agreed to marry, Lord Jack had to tell me the whole. I had taken him for a Frenchman, I must admit, and I was very surprised to learn that he was English. And the brother of a duke, too. I would have expected such a great family to be higher in the instep. But perhaps English aristocrats do not hold themselves aloof in the way that...er..." He coloured and faltered to a halt.

"In the way that French aristocrats do, you mean, Father?" Suzanne said, a little frostily. "Or perhaps we should say 'as they did', for most of them ended up in the arms of Madame Guillotine. And very few of them were mourned."

There was a great deal of bitterness in her words, Ben thought. What could have caused such a reaction? Had the Grolier family suffered in the past at the hands of some domineering French aristocrat? If that were the case, might Suzanne refuse to marry Ben once she discovered who he was?

It was quite likely that the little curé knew that Ben was a viscount's heir. The man must not be allowed to tell Suzanne. That was something for Ben to do himself. Once he had found the right moment.

"Suzanne has been trying to arrange for me to leave for Spain, Father," Ben said quickly, determined to change the subject. Since Jack had trusted the little priest, Ben would do so, too. "Unfortunately, transport is a problem. All the horses in Lyons seem to have been requisitioned."

"That is so everywhere, my son," the curé said. "Why, even in Paris—"

He was interrupted by a knock at the door. It was Guillaume, bringing the wine, and food, though this time the old servant waited outside until Ben bade him enter.

"Thank you, Guillaume," Suzanne said. "Put it on the table, please. Then, if you have seen to the good father's donkey, please lock up the shop and the front of the house. We want no more visitors today."

Guillaume glanced suspiciously at Ben, but then he nodded to Suzanne and left without a word. It was clear that the man distrusted Ben, but it seemed he was prepared to rely on the priest to protect his mistress. Ben tried to tell himself that such loyalty was to be valued in a servant. Perhaps Guillaume would conquer his dislike of Ben once he and Suzanne were safely married?

Suzanne poured the wine and handed a glass to the little priest.

He swallowed a huge mouthful and sighed with pleasure. "Ah, that's better. The dust of the road does get in a man's throat." Suzanne immediately topped up his glass again. He smiled his thanks and turned to Ben. "So you are to go to Spain, sir? How do you plan to do that?"

"To be honest," Ben admitted, "I don't know yet. If we can get hold of a horse, I might have a chance. If we could hire two horses, I could take Suzanne with me."

"But I—" Suzanne began.

The curé held up a hand and gave a little shake of his head. Suzanne sank back to the floor beside his chair, bowed her head and said nothing more. The priest sipped slowly at his wine and frowned up at Ben. "I can see that it would be safer for you, sir, to be riding with a Frenchwoman. Travelling alone, you would be assumed to be a man avoiding enlistment. You would certainly be questioned. And as soon as the authorities heard your foreign accent, you would be arrested. Whereas with Suzanne…" He let his words tail off, but his accusation was clear. Ben was hoping to use Suzanne to save his skin.

"You mistake, sir," Ben objected hotly. "That was not my intention at all. I…I…" Oh dear. This was all going wrong. He ran a hand through his hair and knelt down beside Suzanne. "Forgive me, my love. I have not had a chance to ask you this." He took her cold hand in both of his. "You said we could not be married here in Lyons because it is too dangerous. And you were right. But I dare not leave for England until I have given you the protection of my name. If you would come with me to Spain, we could be safely married as soon as we crossed the border. And I could hire Spanish guards to escort you back here. You would not be gone for long, and Berthe and Guillaume would be able look after your mama. What do you say, love? Will you come with me?"

Suzanne raised her head to look into his face. Her glorious eyes were glistening with unshed tears. "We have not secured even one horse yet, far less two," she said throatily. "And leaving mama for so long…" She shook her head sadly. "Even to keep you safe, Ben, I don't think I could do what you ask."

"But that's not why I—"

Father Bertrand stopped Ben's outraged protest with a kindly hand on his shoulder. "Peace, my son. No one is accusing you of cowardice. You are guilty of something totally different, I think. Very poor planning. Did you really imagine Suzanne could return to Lyons with a Spanish escort and then be safe here? Spain is the enemy of France, remember."

Oh. The priest was right, of course. Ben had allowed his hopes to get the better of his reason. His so-called plan was useless. On their earlier missions, the Aikenhead Honours had always had a meticulous plan, drawn up by Dominic, or by Leo. Jack and Ben had usually contributed little, apart from leg-work. On their first solo mission, here in France, Jack had managed to escape to England, but only because he'd been helped by Marguerite and the little curé.

Ben sighed and bent his head. On his own, in enemy country, he seemed to be a liability. And a danger to anyone who helped him.

Father Bertrand chuckled. "But I have a better plan." He plucked his hat from the floor and dropped it on to Ben's head. "There. It's a perfect fit. I take that as a sign from *le bon dieu.*"

Ben frowned up at the curé. What on earth was he talking about?

Suzanne glanced sideways and began to giggle. "It suits you," she said.

Father Bertrand reached for their joined hands. "You will ride to Spain disguised as a priest. You may take my donkey. He is small, but he is strong and he will not let you down. You will not be challenged. No one would dream of accusing a priest of avoiding army service. As for the accent… Hmm, yes, that might still present something of a problem. We do need a plausible story to explain the accent."

Ben's mind had begun to work again. At last. "I am a German priest. Father Benn. I am on my way to Spain to help a group of wounded German soldiers who were left behind by Wellington's army last year. They have all lost limbs so they are no threat to France. Besides, who could object to a man of God on a mission of mercy? I shall be...er...exceedingly saintly." He made the sign of the cross in the air.

The curé retrieved his hat and beamed at Ben. "As a priest, you will be trying the patience of the good Lord, I can see."

"It is a splendid plan, Father," Suzanne said, rising and pulling Ben to his feet as she did so. "But what about clothes? Ben is much, er, much taller than you are."

"I can let him have a clerical shirt and my cape. Plus my hat, naturally. But he will need a cassock. Do you think you could make one, Suzanne? You will have mine to serve as a pattern. Mine may be slightly larger round the middle," he added, with another chuckle, "but the collar and the buttoning are standard."

Suzanne nodded determinedly. "Of course I can. I think there is some black cloth in the shop store. I should be able to use that, provided there is enough. I don't want to be seen buying black cloth, not unless I absolutely have to. The shopkeepers would assume we'd had a bereavement and start asking questions."

The curé nodded. "Very wise, my dear, very wise. And while you are busy cutting and stitching, I will give this young man some much-needed lessons in how to behave as a priest."

Ben grinned down at the little curé. He was beginning to like the man very much indeed. And he fully understood, now, why Jack had come to trust him.

Suzanne made for the door. "I had best get started." She sounded very businesslike. "I shall be back to take your measurements as soon as I find the cloth."

"Wait, love." Ben caught her by the hand. He glanced back over his shoulder and saw that the little curé was nodding and smiling at him. Encouraged, Ben took a deep breath and said, "Father Bertrand married Jack and Marguerite. I know that he does not have a parish here in Lyons but... Father, before I leave, is it possible for you to marry us? Here? In secret?"

The priest rose from his chair and clasped his hands over his ample middle. He beamed at them both and said, simply, "But certainly, my son. I have been wondering when you would ask."

• • • •

Ben continued stroking the tender skin at the side of his wife's breast. In spite of everything, he seemed intent on rousing her passion. He had his reasons, she supposed. It was, after all, their wedding night and he was the most generous of husbands. Tomorrow he would don his priest's cassock and be gone.

The new Lady Dexter was not about to succumb without a fight. She tiptoed her fingers lazily across the tops of Ben's thighs, venturing occasionally on to the sensitive skin of his belly. Never any lower. That would come in a moment, but a little more wifely torture—in the shape of the things she would *not* do—was a delicious preliminary. He was beginning to writhe against the sheets. It was most gratifying.

"You deceived me." His voice began normally, but ended in a gasp when Suzanne ran the edge of her fingernail down his hard length.

"I did not, sir. You assumed I was a merchant's daughter. If you had asked me outright, I would have told you my mama is the widow of the Marquis de Jerbeaux." She paused, reflecting on that. "Well, I probably would have. Besides, my deception was no worse than yours. I am an aristocrat's daughter. You are a viscount's heir. We love each other to distraction. So I think we are equal, do not you?"

"You are more than equal when it comes to inflicting torture on your poor husband, my lady. It is time, I fancy, for a little retribution." He flicked her onto her back and began to kiss his way slowly down her body, inch by tantalising inch. He lingered lovingly over her breasts until she was moaning and gasping out his name. Then down, down, to her navel and the tender skin of her belly and her inner thighs. And finally to the core of her.

Suzanne felt herself soaring as his rhythm caught her and carried her aloft. She heard the sound of her own cry and the world shattered around her.

• • • •

Ben pulled her into the crook of his arm and dropped a kiss on to her hair.

She frowned up at him. "But you...?"

He stroked the damp curls back from her forehead. "I can wait, wife. We are agreed, are we not, that I must not get you with child?" He had gloried in her pleasure. He told himself that that was more than enough compensation for his own lack of fulfilment.

She snuggled into his side and put her arm around his middle. Soon she would fall asleep, he hoped. It was a kind of torture to have her here in his bed and to be unable to love her fully, as a husband should. But it was what he had to do. To keep her safe.

"Mmm," she breathed against his skin. "I feel so...so cherished. I love you, Lord Dexter."

"And I love you, too, my lady. But you should sleep now. You have all those buttons to sew onto my cassock tomorrow, remember?" He grinned wickedly at her.

"I am not sleepy. I want to— That is, I am a wife now, and I want to satisfy my husband, as he has satisfied me."

"Suzanne, you know that it is not safe for me to—"

She silenced him by putting a finger across his lips. "Hush, love. I know that. But surely there are other ways?" She was starting to blush delightfully, but she seemed very determined. Her fingers were beginning to stray down over his belly.

Ben groaned. This was another kind of torture altogether.

121

She went very slowly. Her every touch, every squeeze, every stroke sent the blood rioting round his body and roused him even more. He closed his eyes and clutched at the sheets. Higher and higher. Nearer and nearer. He was clawing towards the light. It was too far.

Then her mouth was on his. And the moment came. His groan was swallowed in her long, passionate kiss.

Afterwards, he lay speechless for a long time, staring up into the darkness and marvelling at the wonder that was the wife he held in his arms. She was beautiful, and she loved him.

But tomorrow he was going to leave her.

He had done everything he could to keep her safe. She had the proof of their marriage carefully hidden, along with a letter from Ben to his grandfather, explaining everything. If Ben should die on the journey back to England, Suzanne would be able to claim her rightful place. Father Bertrand would stand by her. And so would Jack, Ben was sure.

This time, he had a good plan. Father Benn, the German priest, would make his way to Spain, riding his stout little donkey. Then Father Benn would disappear, to be replaced by Baron Dexter, the rich English aristocrat. Once he made it to the coast, his gold would buy him a swift passage to England.

No, Ben had absolutely no intention of dying. Not now, when he had so much to live for.

Chapter Eighteen

"IT IS OVER, MISTRESS," Guillaume announced as soon as he returned from the market. "All Lyons is buzzing with the news." He was hot and sweaty. And he seemed very upset, too.

Suzanne took one look at the lines of strain on his face and her mouth dried. Her heart began to race. This news must be very bad. "What has happened? For God's sake, tell me."

"There was a great battle. In the middle of June. Near Brussels. Some little place called Waterloo." His voice cracked and he looked round the kitchen for something to drink. There was a carafe of watered wine on the table. He poured some into a tumbler and drank greedily.

Suzanne did not understand what he was talking about. "But that was weeks ago. Why have we not heard before?"

"It is not the kind of news that Bonaparte wanted to spread. Especially as the armies died in their thousands. On both sides." Guillaume shook his head, his eyes troubled. "All those brave young men, cut down." He wiped his forehead and took another large gulp of wine.

Why was he not telling her the one thing that really mattered? "Yes, but who won?" she asked impatiently.

"I told you, mistress. It is over. The Allies won. Wellington and Blücher. Bonaparte fled back to Paris. Apparently he tried to abdicate in favour of his son, but the Allies were having none of it. In the market, they are saying that King Louis has already returned to Paris and Bonaparte is to be exiled."

"Back to Elba?"

Guillaume snorted and shook his head again. "I doubt it. The English are in charge now. I imagine they will send Bonaparte as far as possible from France. They won't want another escape. Especially when it creates such carnage."

Suzanne had been so intent on questioning the old servant about the outcome of the battle that she had not been listening properly to anything else. "What do you mean, 'carnage'?" she managed, in a horrified whisper.

"They died by the thousands and tens of thousands, mistress. And thousands more lost legs, or arms, or eyes. The Allies were victorious, right enough, but the cost was enormous. On both sides." His voice cracked and he tossed down the rest of his wine. "So many families will be in mourning, royalists and Bonapartists alike. Poor stricken France. Every village will have lost sons."

And every village in England, too? Suzanne could not will away that terrible thought. Fear gripped her like red-hot pincers. Her heart began to beat very fast. What if Ben had gone to join Wellington's army? Might he be one of the fallen? Among those piles of battered, bloody corpses?

For a moment, she could not breathe. She was going to faint. She grabbed the kitchen table for support.

"Mistress? Are you unwell?" Guillaume helped her to a chair. He poured wine for her and forced her to drink a little.

His gruff concern brought her back to reality. She was panicking, allowing her fears for Ben to get the better of her reason. It was impossible for him to have reached England by the middle of June, far less Brussels. At best, he might have reached the Spanish coast and boarded a ship for England. He couldn't have been with Wellington's army. He couldn't. There had not been time.

Nevertheless, she offered up a fervent prayer for Ben's safety. And another that he would return for her soon.

124

She took another sip of wine. "Tell me what else you learned, Guillaume." She was forcing herself to sound stronger than she felt.

"The royalists here are cock-a-hoop, obviously," Guillaume said. "You'd be amazed how many more have emerged from the woodwork. Half of them turncoats, I can guarantee it," he added, in a voice full of scorn. "They kept their heads down before. Now they're planning revenge attacks on anyone who might be a Bonapartist. Or a republican. Cowards, and bullies, the lot of them. There will be fighting in the streets, you mark my words, mistress."

Now, when she had every reason to panic, she did not. Faced with the prospect of rampaging mobs in the city streets, she calmly laid out her plans and gave her orders. "We will have no part in such wickedness. We will close the business until order is restored. However long it takes. Make sure all the street doors are securely barred, Guillaume, and all the windows shuttered. We have plenty of provisions, and water from our own well, so no one needs to leave the house. Go now and see to it. Quickly. I will warn Berthe to keep mama close."

Guillaume nodded eagerly. "I will turn the house into a fortress in no time, mistress. And I have your father's pistols. If anyone tries to attack us, I will shoot them."

• • • •

Dover, England

It was nearly midnight when the mud-spattered chaise drew up outside the Duke of Calder's house near Dover's fortified harbour. Ben flung himself down on to the flagway before the postilions had even had time to dismount. "You've made much better time than I expected." He reached into his pocket for the extra guineas he had prepared. "And I did promise you'd be well rewarded for speed. Here."

The older postilion's eyes widened as he saw how much money he was to be given. "Thank you, sir. My lord, I mean." He touched his cap, but Ben was already up the steps and hammering the knocker.

It was Jack who opened the door. His jaw dropped. "Good Lord! Ben!"

Ben had been unable to believe his luck when he'd learned, at the last posting inn, that the famous Duke of Calder had changed horses there, little more than an hour earlier. His luck was holding, it seemed, for at least one Aikenhead brother was still on dry land. Ben might not have to make his own way to France, after all. Finding Jack reduced to the role of butler was an unexpected bonus, though. Ben couldn't help chuckling. "Can't afford servants any more, eh? The Aikenheads must really have fallen on hard times."

"What? Oh, very funny." Jack was not smiling. He pulled the door wide and stood back. "You'd better come in," he said tightly. "The others will be relieved to hear that our long-lost wanderer has returned."

"Wanderer?" Ben echoed.

Jack stooped to heft Ben's valise inside. When he stood up again, his face looked drawn. "I'd given you up for dead, you numbskull," he muttered, closing the door.

"But—" Before Ben could say another word, Jack enveloped him in a bear hug. Seconds later, they were grinning at each other like a pair of village idiots.

"Where the devil have you been all this time?" Jack began. "And how is it—"

"You were supposed to answer the door, brat, not host a salon." The voice came from the gloom at the back of the hallway.

"Dominic!" Ben exclaimed. "You're back."

"As you see. Welcome to Dover." Dominic clapped Ben on the shoulder as they shook hands. "Leo is here, too. We're off to France in a few hours. Just waiting for the tide."

126

"Are you? That's another stroke of luck for me, then. May I—?"

"You may do many things, Ben, but not here in the hall. Come into the saloon and have a glass of wine. I dare say you could do with a bite to eat, too?"

"Well…yes. But if you have no servants here—"

Dominic's lips twitched. "The house has been shut up for months and we had no time to send for the servants. But my valet can turn his hand to most things. Jack, ask Cooper to see what he can rustle up by way of supper, will you?"

Jack charged off in the direction of the servants' quarters, while Dominic ushered Ben into the blue saloon. Some of the furniture was still under holland covers, but there were decanters and glasses on the table in front of the fireplace and a small fire in the grate. Leo turned from warming his hands and beamed a welcome at Ben. "Glad to see you've made it at last, wanderer."

"Blister it, Leo, not you as well? I'll have you know I haven't *wandered* anywhere. I followed Jack's orders and came back by the most direct route, through Spain. If there was any wandering done, it was by that blasted ship on the way to Southampton. The captain blamed it on contrary winds, but—"

"Never mind that," Dominic said curtly. "You're here now. What news have you from Lyons?"

Before Ben could respond, there was more hammering on the front door.

"Now what?" The duke sounded exasperated.

Leo quietly left the saloon.

Ben heard low voices in the hall. Then Leo returned with a packet in his hand. "One of the grooms from the Park. Sent by mama with this. I've told him to wait, in case we need to send an answer."

Leo handed over the packet and Dominic ripped it open, just as Jack returned to the saloon and said, "Cooper promises to bring supper as soon as he's—" He stopped dead, staring at the letter in the duke's hand. "Now what?"

Ben laughed. Jack was most definitely Dominic's brother. They looked alike, of course. But the two of them even sounded alike, some of the time. It felt very good to be back among such friends and comrades.

Dominic was scanning the papers he held. "It's a note from mama. Enclosing a letter that arrived for her by express from London. Mama says... Ah, yes. She does not know who the letter is from, because she cannot decipher a word of it, beyond the first few lines. But as it seemed to be urgent, she decided to send it on in hopes that her groom would reach us before we sailed. Her man must have galloped like the wind to get here so quickly." He looked up. "Where did you leave him, Leo? He'll be needing to get the dust out of his throat after a ride like that."

"Already done, Ace. Sent him to Cooper in the kitchen."

"Of course you did." Dominic nodded his thanks to his second in command. "And now to this urgent letter. Let's hope it is good news." With his brothers looking over his shoulders, he began to read it aloud. *"Madam, I take the liberty of writing to you, since I am unsure of where your sons may be at present. I would deem it a favour if you would*—" He stopped, frowned and peered more closely at the paper. "I cannot make out another word of it, either. Mama was right. An appalling scrawl. Even the signature is indecipherable."

Ben was sure he must have turned as red as a beetroot. He opened his mouth to explain that the letter was his.

Jack was too quick for him. "I know that scribbled fist. It belongs to Ben here." Jack chortled and grinned mischievously at Ben. "Being left-handed makes things worse, obviously. And when he's in a rush, poor chap, his writing goes all over the place." Totally ignoring Ben's protests, Jack took the paper from Dominic and squinted at it.

"If you wish to know what my letter says, I suggest you let me read it to you." Ben was hoping to recover his dignity, but he was not at all sure that he was going to succeed. Not against Jack's wicked sense of humour.

He was right. Jack was holding the paper well out of Ben's reach. Leo was grinning. Even Dominic was not managing to keep a straight face.

"Hmm. Even I can't read it all, I'm afraid, but it definitely says that Suzanne and the marquise were both well, and safe, in Lyons. Apart from that, I'm not sure what..." Jack frowned and moved the paper closer to the candles. "Oh, now I see. *That's* why you scribbled this in such a hurry. You were dashing off to your grandfather's place. To get more blunt, I suppose?"

"Yes, I had to—"

"Wait a bit, though," Jack cut in again. "I do believe that this word here—" he waved the letter at Leo, pointing with his finger "—might be *marauder*. Did you have marauders in Lyons, Ben? Did you have to repel boarders with cold steel? Cutlasses and such?"

Ben finally managed to snatch the letter out of Jack's fingers. He drew himself up. "The word is not *marauder*, as you know perfectly well, Jack Aikenhead. The word is *married*."

"Is it really?" Jack made to reach for the letter, as if to check. His question sounded innocent, but his dancing eyes betrayed him. "Married, eh?"

"Yes, married, you muttonhead. Suzanne and I were married before I left for Spain. By Father Bertrand, as it happens. The good father who married you and Marguerite, too, I believe?"

"Oh, Lord." Jack's grin had disappeared in an instant. He now looked distinctly deflated. "Marguerite. She doesn't know. I need to—" He ran a hand through his hair. "Oh, Lord," he said again.

"Let that be a lesson to you, brat, on the perils of taking your jokes too far. May I suggest you write a note to your wife, giving her this excellent news? Make sure it's legible, though. We want no more misunderstandings. Mama's groom can take it back to the Park. And, in the meantime, Leo and I will give Ben your hearty congratulations, as well as our own."

Both Dominic and Leo shook Ben warmly by the hand. He accepted their good wishes but his impatience was clear. "If you're sailing for France, Dominic, will you take me along? I've been away for weeks now and heavens knows what's happening in Lyons since Bonaparte's defeat. I swore to Suzanne that I would return for her. But with no news from me, she is bound to be fretting. If you could land me on French soil, I should be able to make my own way from there. M'grandfather came up with plenty of blunt once he knew that I had another mission in France."

Leo chuckled but said nothing.

"I'm delighted to hear you are so plump in the pocket, Ben. And I will happily convey you to France."

"Thank you, Ace. You are a good friend."

"We might perhaps travel together?"

"Certainly. Has Wellington sent for you? Are you bound for Paris?"

"Not exactly. We thought, a little further… Perhaps Lyons?"

Jack, listening from the table where he was writing his letter, spoiled the duke's straight-faced jest with a gasp of laughter.

"Why, you…you devils. You are all roasting me. Do you tell me you were already bound for Lyons? To save Suzanne and her mother?"

"Of course we were, Ben. Suzanne is sister to Jack's wife, remember. So they are family. And since you have married Suzanne, I have to say that you are family now, too. Whether you will it or no, Ben Dexter, you are become one of the Aikenheads. And the Honours will always defend their own."

Ben let out a shaky breath. His shoulders relaxed. "Thank you, Ace. I have always felt myself as almost one of you. And now, truly, it seems that I am."

Jack finished sealing his letter and came across to shake Ben's hand. "Congratulations, brother. On all counts." He was grinning from ear to ear. "You couldn't have found a better way of joining the family."

The door opened to admit Cooper, carrying a laden tray.

"Splendid. Here is supper." The duke motioned to his valet to put the tray on the table and take Jack's note. "Give that to the groom, Cooper. He's to deliver it as soon as he gets back to the Park."

The valet bowed and left.

"And then, I think, we should all take what rest we can. We must be on board in good time for we dare not miss another tide. We have a long journey ahead of us." The duke paused a moment before adding, "And, God willing, a successful rescue at the end of it."

Chapter Nineteen

AFTER WELL OVER A WEEK of chaos on the streets, and precious little sleep, Guillaume was looking haggard. He seemed to have aged years since the news of France's defeat. "There were pockets of rioting all over Lyons last night," he reported, his face grim, when he returned from venturing outside. "The Bonapartists have nothing to lose now and they're fighting tooth and nail. The royalist factions have started fighting each other, too. All sorts of stupid allegations about who resisted Bonaparte and who did not." The old man shook his head in disgust.

Suzanne was trying very hard not to let her fears show. She was the head of this little household. Father Bertrand had long since returned to Rouen, so it was up to Suzanne to keep everyone safe until Ben arrived to take them to England. *One day at a time.* That was her motto and she had been repeating it to herself, over and over. With each passing day that House Grolier stayed safe from the rioters, they were one day closer to Ben's arrival.

"And now there's a new danger. Houses were set on fire last night. Some folk reckon it was deliberate. Enemies settling old scores."

Suzanne gasped. "But there were no fires in this part of town, surely?"

"No, mistress. They were all up on the hill. Even the hotheads are not stupid enough to start a fire down here in the old town. If a single house went up in flames here, we would all be doomed, crammed together as we are. Thousands could die."

Suzanne shivered. They had no defence against fire. Fire in the old town would be utterly devastating. "We must take what precautions we can, Guillaume. Fill all the available buckets with water and put them in the hallway by the main door. If someone sets a fire, it will start there."

Guillaume nodded. "And I'll bring a pallet down here and sleep in the hall. If I stay sleeping upstairs, I might be too late." He made a face and started for the back of the house, where the buckets were kept.

Guillaume was right. Someone had to be on hand to put out a fire, the moment it started. No matter how tired he was, he would fight to save the family. He was the only defence they had.

Oh Ben, please come soon. Please, my love. I feel so alone. And I am afraid of what the mob might do to us.

Suzanne swallowed hard and smoothed her hands over her apron. Time to get to work. She had to concentrate on the day-to-day business of survival. There were chores to be done if they were all to eat.

• • • •

It was getting late when the knocking began. Suzanne was sitting with her mother, in order to give old Berthe a break and a chance to eat her supper. The marquise's eyelids were drooping, perhaps because she had taken more wine than usual with her meal. Soon, she would fall asleep, and Suzanne could steal away.

The knocking on the main door turned into heavy pounding.

The marquise shot upright and cried out, "The *canaille*. They are coming for us."

"No, Mama, no. You are safe here. No one can get in. The doors are stoutly barred and Guillaume is downstairs with his pistols. You are safe. I promise."

The hammer blows continued. Suzanne cursed under her breath. She needed to stay here to pacify her poor, frightened mama. But she also needed to be downstairs, taking charge of whatever was happening there. If the rioters were trying to break in, Guillaume could not defend the house all by himself.

Berthe rushed in, carrying a fire bucket in one hand and a cudgel in the other. "There's all sorts of ruffians in the street below," she gasped. "Right nasty looking fellows. A whole mob of 'em. Guillaume says you're to come down at once. Don't worry. I'll stay with *madame*."

The marquise was starting to shake.

Berthe sat down beside her charge and put a comforting arm round the marquise's shoulders. She waved Suzanne towards the door. "Go on now. Nothin' you can do here."

Suzanne gulped and ran for the door. Downstairs, the banging continued. The men outside were shouting, too, though she couldn't make out any of the words. At this rate, the mob would soon break down the door. But who were they? Why were they picking on the Grolier household? Why now, after weeks of being ignored?

Suzanne raced into Marguerite's room, the room that had been Ben's. It overlooked the main street. She should be able to squint through the gap in the shutters. She would at least discover how many of them there were.

What she saw made her stomach lurch and her heart race. A mob of men—a dozen at least—carrying sticks and burning flambeaux. A couple of empty wagons. Were they planning to break down the door and rob the house? Guillaume's pistols would be precious little use against so many.

Suzanne closed her eyes for a second and offered up a tiny prayer.

"Open the door!"

That shouted command was clear enough. But the man's French accent was not local.

Suzanne pushed the shutter open a fraction and peered down. The gang of men had spread out into a defensive half-circle round the wagons. By the door, there was a group of four more. She was looking down on three dark heads. And one fair.

Her heart stopped. *Could it be?*

"Ben?" she managed, at last.

All four heads jerked up to look for the source of the voice.

"Suzanne, is that you?" Ben's beloved voice cried.

Joy flooded her whole being. He was here. *He was.* She pushed the shutter wide and leaned out so that he could see her. In a moment, he was grinning up at her. He looked quite wonderful. He had promised to come back for her and now he was here. And it seemed he had brought a private army, too.

She sagged on to the window sill, as relief overwhelmed her and sapped the strength from her legs. But her inner voice was urging her to sing at the top of her voice and to dance round the room. Her husband, her darling Ben, had returned to rescue them all.

One of the unknown dark-haired men bowed up to Suzanne and said, with the utmost courtesy, "Good evening, ma'am. We apologise for arriving unannounced, and at such a late hour, but we have brought you your husband. He is very keen to see you. Might we come in?"

Suzanne was so struck by his bizarre politeness that she began to laugh and laugh. Ben was here. Lord Jack, too. And the two other dark-haired gentlemen must be Lord Jack's brothers. It was the miracle she had been praying for. Ben was here. And everyone would be safe at last.

"Suzanne, do stop giggling and open the door. We're getting very thirsty out here." When nothing happened, Ben gave the door another couple of hefty thumps. "Are you in there, Guillaume? Open the door, there's a good fellow. Your mistress seems incapable of descending the stairs."

Suzanne managed to control herself enough to go out on to the landing and call down to the old servant, "You may open the door, Guillaume. It is my husband. And Marguerite's, too. We have nothing to fear any more."

A moment later, she heard the bolts being drawn back, and booted feet in the passageway. She flung herself down the stairs and into her husband's arms.

• • • •

Suzanne was losing herself in his kiss, melting into his beloved body. It was as if their souls were beginning to join.

Ben threaded his fingers into her hair and began to deepen the kiss even more. Suzanne responded eagerly. Often and often during these past lonely weeks, she had dreamed of how it would be when he returned, but this was so much more. This was no fleeting fantasy. This was vibrant, breathing reality. Oh, it was heaven.

A cough shattered the silence. A very deliberate cough.

"Oh." Suzanne broke away from Ben. What on earth had they been thinking of? Kissing—kissing passionately, too—in a hallway full of people? A wave of heat engulfed her. She knew she must be bright scarlet with embarrassment.

She hardly dared to raise her eyes. But then someone took her hand and lifted it to his lips. It was not Ben. She knew it was not his touch.

"Lady Dexter, your servant." It was Lord Jack. He straightened and let go of her hand. When she looked up at him, she saw that there was a very mischievous glint in his eye, even though he was trying hard to look serious. "Or perhaps I may call you by name, as we are brother and sister now?"

"What? Oh. Oh yes, of course," she stammered. For it was true. Lord Jack Aikenhead—Jack, now—was her brother, married to her sister. "Marguerite…?" she began uncertainly.

"Marguerite is well, never fear. She sends her fondest love, to you and to your mama. She also bade me bring you to England with all speed. All of you," he added, looking round to find Guillaume. The servant was standing among the fire buckets, with one pistol loose in his hand and another tucked into his belt. On his face there was an expression of bewilderment as he gazed first at one, then another of these imposing newcomers. Suzanne saw at a glance that Jack's older brothers were men to be reckoned with, even though they were waiting quietly in the shadows by the door, allowing the men she knew to take the lead.

Jack grinned across at the old servant. "I fancy I owe you an apology, Guillaume," he said airily. "For deceiving you."

The old man muttered something inaudible.

Ben stepped between them and grasped Guillaume's hand. He shook it vigorously. "I owe you more than I can ever repay, Guillaume." He gestured towards the pistols. "You have kept the ladies safe, when I could not. Thank you."

"Only doing my duty, sir," Guillaume said gruffly. "My lord, I should say." He tucked the second pistol into his belt. "I have served *madame* since before she was a bride. I will always serve her family."

Ben smiled and clapped the man on the shoulder. "And the family will always need you, and value you," he said solemnly. "Just at this moment, we need you to prepare for departure. At first light tomorrow."

"But we cannot—" Suzanne began, shocked. Did he expect her to abandon everything they had built here? Surely not? Besides, it would take time to convince mama of the need to leave her home.

"Hush, love. We must." Ben took her hand and drew her to him. "Dominic will explain. Dominic?"

"Lady Dexter." The Duke of Calder stepped out of the shadow. He was almost the image of Lord Jack. Almost, but not quite. They had the same features, and the same black hair and deep blue eyes, but the duke was taller, and broader in the shoulder than Jack. And the duke was clearly a man used to command. He bowed to Suzanne. "Calder, at your service, ma'am." He waved the fourth man forward.

"Before we discuss plans, may I present my next brother, Leo?"

Lord Leo did not share his brothers' dramatically dark colouring, and yet, to Suzanne, he instantly seemed far more compelling than either of them. Leo had dallied with many a woman's heart, Ben said. Now that Suzanne had met him, she understood. He had that indefinable allure that would draw every female eye. The woman who had tamed such a rake must be very special indeed.

Lord Leo bowed, very elegantly. "Servant, Lady Dexter."

Suzanne curtseyed as best she could, since Ben was still holding her close.

The duke smoothly took charge. "The truth is, Lady Dexter, that Lyons is not safe for any of us. If the men of Lyons discover they have English invaders in their midst, we may have a battle on our hands. We have brought men with us, but not nearly enough to withstand an army of angry locals. Not without bloodshed."

When Suzanne did not respond immediately, he frowned and spoke more sharply. "We are here solely to protect you and your household. Not to start a new war. By far our best strategy is to leave before the potential opposition learns what we are about. You do see that, do you not?"

Suzanne felt the pressure of Ben's fingers on hers. Clearly, he wanted her to agree to the duke's proposal. And she could see that it was all eminently sensible. But it gave her no time to think, to reconcile herself to the loss of everything she knew. She put her hand to her mouth and screwed her eyes shut. She said the first thing that occurred to her. "I do not think mama will wish to go."

To her surprise, Lord Jack laughed. "Have no worries on that score, sister. Leave it to Dominic."

• • • •

It was decided. They were to leave at dawn, as Ben had said. They had time—just—to pack for the journey, but

138

they must travel light. And there was much else to be done, so there was no time to be wasted in talking. Or worrying.

One of the wagons was needed for the duke's little army of stalwarts, with their weapons. Willing hands quickly loaded the second wagon with the stock of Grolier silk and a few of the family's personal possessions—small roped boxes for Suzanne and the servants, and a larger trunk for the marquise who might be upset if forced to part with any of the vast array of mementos that surrounded her every day.

Suzanne scurried upstairs to pack a box for Marguerite, too. Her sister would not need the clothes she had left behind, but there were favourite books, and trinkets, and other treasures that she would not want to lose.

Jack was before her. There was an empty valise on Marguerite's bed. And Jack had been running his hands through his hair again. "Suzanne. Thank goodness." He waved a piece of paper in the air. "Marguerite gave me a list of things to collect for her, but I can't find half of them."

Suzanne chuckled. "No, I dare say you can't. Why not let me do it?" She whisked the paper out of his fingers and glanced down her sister's list. "Yes, I can find all of these. Leave it to me."

"Bless you, sister," he said, dropping a kiss on her cheek.

"Unhand my wife, my lord, or I shall have to call you out."

Suzanne whirled round. Ben was standing in the doorway, grinning evilly at them both. He was clearly enjoying himself, the wretch. Did these men take nothing seriously? Even when all their lives were in danger?

"Oh, go away, do," Suzanne said impatiently, flapping a hand a him. "Have you nothing better to do than disturb others at their work? We have to leave in a few hours, and mama is still—"

Ben stopped her with a raised hand. "Madam wife," he began pompously, "it is time you learned to have faith in the Aikenhead Honours. Jack told you, did he not, that Dominic would resolve everything? And so he has. Your mama will be ready to travel in the morning. Indeed, she is eager to be off."

"What? But how?"

Ben grinned. "Dominic is a great planner, as you will discover. He made us tell him all about the marquise and her…er…difficulties. And he worked out a solution. He brought one of his grand ducal carriages across to France with us. He invited your mama to travel in style, escorted by her family and servants, and with a duke's crest on the door. She was perfectly content to accept. She sees it as a return to the proper deference she received in her youth. Apparently, she believes it is no more than her due to be escorted by one of England's foremost dukes."

Jack shook his head, grinning. "So it did work. I wasn't sure it would. Trust Dominic to find a way. He could always out-think all the rest of us."

Suzanne was speechless. It was so simple. And yet so very clever.

"Once you have finished packing for Marguerite, love, I suggest you lie down on your bed for an hour or two." Ben nodded nonchalantly towards the now-empty silk store and Suzanne's bedchamber, beyond. "It is already late and tomorrow will be a very long day."

Suzanne was not deceived. Not in the least. The silk store held gloriously tempting memories, for both of them. Ben was deliberately reminding her of delights past, and delights to come. "As you say, husband," she replied demurely. "But surely you should rest, too?"

Behind her, Jack chortled. Then he made for the door, clapping Ben on the shoulder as he passed. "I think, old man, that I am decidedly *de trop* in this conversation." He clattered down the stairs, still laughing.

Chapter Twenty

BEN GAZED DOWN AT his beautiful, sleeping wife. She was an amazing woman—courageous, and determined—a match for any man. She had worked so hard these last months and years to keep her little family together. There was nothing she would not tackle, for them, when it was necessary. Even if her life was at stake.

One of her hands was lying on the pillow by her cheek. It was not the hand of a noble lady, but of a working woman. The skin was red and chapped in places, and two of the fingernails were broken. No wonder, given all the chores she had had to do since he left, even when she was not weaving at her loom. Ben resolved that, as soon as he had her safely back in England, she would be waited on, hand and foot, like a pampered oriental princess. Suzanne's poor worn hands would soon be as smooth and white and soft as a great lady's should be.

All the better to stroke across a husband's naked skin.

That thought, once in his mind, would not be banished. The effect on his body was so arousing that he considered, for a moment, whether he should leave his wife to sleep alone. If he climbed into the bed beside her, as was his right, would he have the strength of will to leave her to sleep?

Sleep was what she must need. Desperately. It was probable that she had not slept soundly in all the weeks he had been gone, for she had all the cares of the household on her slender shoulders, and always that lurking uncertainty about whether her husband would live to return to her. Such terrible burdens for her to have borne alone.

He would slide into the bed beside her and take her into his arms, to hold her while she slept. She would sleep the sounder, he told himself, knowing that he was there to protect her. And he? He would simply hold her. Nothing more than that. There would be plenty of opportunities for lovemaking in the days and weeks to come, once he had her safe. They were man and wife. They had a lifetime together ahead of them.

He snuffed his candle and stripped off his clothes in the dark, listening all the while to the sound of her slow breathing. It did not change at all, not even when he lifted the edge of the bedcovers and slid in beside her. Her bed was warm and welcoming against his naked skin. He even thought he detected the faintest scent of summer herbs drifting across the pillow, beckoning him in to join his sleeping wife.

He put his hand to his own cheek. The rest of his body was on fire, but his hands were cold. If he touched her, he was bound to wake her and he must not do that. He tucked both his hands under his body in an effort to warm them. Then he lay quietly, mere inches from his wife's delectable body, and counted off the minutes until he could safely draw her into his arms.

"Mmm." Suzanne stirred in her sleep and rolled towards him while he was still counting. A moment later, she was snuggling into his warmth and slipping an arm around his middle.

He gasped. He could not help it. She was naked.

His sharp intake of breath must have been very loud in the silence, but it did not seem to wake her. Her breathing did not change. Her soft cheek was nestling into his shoulder and one bare breast was resting tantalisingly on his arm.

Such sweet torture.

She had gone to bed naked. For him. Waiting for him. There was no other possible explanation. And that thought was so very arousing. How on earth was he to keep to his resolve? His whole body was clamouring to wake her, to kiss her, to join her body fully with his.

He did nothing. He suffered agonies of frustration, but he forced himself to lie still. He owed it to his beloved wife not to disturb her rest.

He had promised himself he would hold her. Only that.

Roughened fingers began to dance delicately across his buttocks.

"I thought you were asleep," he managed finally. His throat had gone so dry he could barely make a sound. Those wicked stroking fingers....

"I was," she murmured, moving her head a fraction so that her breath was caressing his nipple. "But I promised myself I would wake up as soon as you were here with me. I knew I would. No matter how much you tried not to disturb me." She took his flesh between her teeth and bit down gently. When his only response was a strangled gasp, she began laughing softly, deep in her throat, and raised her head a little. "And you see, husband mine, that I am very much awake, as I intended."

"What I see—or rather, don't see, since I was stupid enough to snuff the candle—is a wonderfully wilful wife, who is possibly a witch. Cast your spells, my love. I have not the least desire to resist you."

He could feel her smiling against his skin. She said nothing, but in a moment she began kissing him. All of him. Slowly and very thoroughly, even down to his toes and the tips of his fingers. Soon every inch of his skin was tingling and alive, desperate to be selected for her next touch. Magical, indeed.

She made a little sound in her throat that might have been a chuckle. Or perhaps she was musing on her next target? Long seconds ticked by, while she neither moved nor touched.

It was too much. Ben groaned aloud. He could not help it. Soon, he would explode.

"Fie, my lord. Did you not tell me, but a moment ago, that you would not resist anything I wished to do?"

"I swear I am not resisting." His voice came out as a strangled croak. "Not. Not resist— Argh!" His control broke completely, the moment she took his erection in her hand and began to squeeze. He needed her desperately. It had to be now. But he had promised…

He put his hands to her waist and lifted her on top of him, settling her slowly until he was fully sheathed in her glorious body. She let out a long sigh of pleasure.

"Not resisting. Not. Need you, my love," he pleaded. "Can't wait much long—"

She bent forward, so that her hair was tickling the skin of his face and neck and shoulders, and silenced him with a long kiss. "Now," she said softly against his mouth, "I think it is time for some exploration of this new…er…" She wiggled her bottom a little. Then she began tightening her muscles around him. Once, and then again, harder. He groaned once more and she laughed, her whole body vibrating. That was more arousing than anything else she had done to him.

Her laughter faded as she caught the rhythm and began to move with him. Faster. Higher. Soon she was gasping for breath, as he was. And then they reached the crest and went over into fulfilment. Together.

• • • •

"You should be sleeping, love," Ben said, not for the first time.

Suzanne snuggled closer into his embrace. This was where she wanted to be. And the feelings were too wonderful for sleep. "Mmm," she murmured, into his skin. "But I'm not."

He chuckled. "I wonder if our marriage will always be like this? I give orders and you…er…"

"Ignore them?" Suzanne finished. "It will depend on the orders, I imagine. I did promise to obey, so I suppose I really ought to do what you tell me. Some of the time, at least," she added, wickedly.

He laughed and kissed her soundly. "I am a very lucky man to have found you, my love. And I will try to ensure that my orders are...er...reasonable. Now that the war is over, we can be together, for I will not be leaving you for spying missions with the Aikenheads. We have been disbanded. With honour, I might add. My task now is to take on the management of the Hoarwithy estate and to make a life in England for my darling wife and—God willing—our children." He kissed her again. "It is a huge step for you, I know. A new life, in a strange country, and a new language, to boot, but you will have Marguerite to help you, as well as the dowager duchess. No regrets, I hope, love?"

Suzanne shook her head, deliberately letting her curls tickle his skin. She felt loved, and cherished. She was where she belonged. "No regrets," she said firmly. "My place is with you. By your side." She dropped a kiss on the corner of his mouth. "And in your bed." She ran the very tip of her tongue along his lower lip. Sleep was the last thing she wanted now. He needed to understand that.

He did. Instantly. He caught up her hands and rolled her under him so that he could settle into the cradle of her hips. "You are a wicked woman, Lady Dexter, to tempt your poor husband so. But I find I have no desire—" he raised his hips and pushed deep into her welcoming warmth "—no desire at all to resist you."

The urge was very strong now, for both of them. He began to move, timing his thrusts to the rhythm of his words as he said her name, over and over. "Suzanne. My love. My life."

• • • •

They had been travelling for hours when Dominic finally called a halt. The sun was high in the sky and it was very

145

hot. Everyone but the marquise was suffering. She, true to her code, refused to acknowledge the inconvenience of the summer heat. Others might sweat and suffer; a marquise did not.

Ben wiped the back of his hand across his forehead and marvelled at his mother-in-law. She looked as cool and collected as she had when they set out, in the relative chill of the dawn air. Dominic's tactics appeared to be working wonderfully well. Being treated like a great lady again seemed to have restored much of her equanimity. And it had taken a huge weight off Suzanne's shoulders, too, for which Ben was very grateful. His wife had borne enough. He wanted to see an end to her worried frowns. He wanted her to be truly carefree, and joyful, and laughing up at a cloudless sky.

"We can break for an hour or so," Dominic said, handing the reins to one of the temporary grooms. "The horses need a breather after that climb."

"And so do the rest of us," Jack said, mopping his face.

"I think you'll find that Leo has matters in hand," Dominic replied calmly.

Leo, in his usual role as brigade major of the Aikenhead Honours, was already marshalling his men into parties to act as lookouts, to see to the horses, and to set out blankets in the shade so that everyone could eat in relative comfort. "Well-chosen spot this," he said, when he came to report to the duke that all was ready. "You can see for miles up here. No enemy could creep up on us."

Dominic smiled. "No, but you've set pickets anyway. Just in case. Very wise."

Leo shrugged. "Pays to be careful." He excused himself to Suzanne and her mother and went to eat with his men. Within ten minutes, the sound of raucous laughter was echoing from the far end of the little camp. Ben guessed that Leo was probably telling some of his more scandalous stories.

It did not take long to finish their makeshift meal and for Suzanne to escort the marquise back to the carriage to rest. "I suggest you do not stray too near to Leo's lads in your meanderings, my love," Ben said when she returned to their little group. "Their talk might be a little, er, ripe for a lady's ears."

Suzanne smiled and joined him on the rug. "English ripe, or French ripe? If it is English, it would not matter, for I would not understand it."

"Oh. No, of course not." He paused, frowning. "I never thought to ask, love. Do you speak English at all?"

"I have some," Suzanne said, trying not to smile. "Marguerite and I were well taught when we were small. Before." She glanced across to the grand ducal carriage. "Mama speaks good English. Or, at least, she did once."

"Your sister's English is very fluent now," the duke said, raising himself on one elbow to reach for his wineglass. "My mother has been helping her to improve. And she will do the same for you, Lady Dexter, if you wish."

"What Dominic means," Jack put in from his place leaning against the tree trunk, "is that our mama is a very managing sort of person. If she decides to take your training in hand, Suzanne, you will find yourself trained, believe me." He shuddered theatrically. Then he brightened. "And if she is cracking the whip over you, she might leave Marguerite in peace. So we'd have more time for other things." He smiled to himself.

"You're painting the dowager as some kind of ogress, Jack," Ben protested. "That really cannot be fair. You said Marguerite was very easy in the dowager's company." He glanced across at his wife. The last thing he wanted was for Suzanne to be anxious about meeting Jack's mother. He said as much. "For the dowager is kindness itself," he finished. "If there is to be a problem once we reach England, it will be with my grandfather," he added quickly, knowing that if he did not warn Suzanne about the old man,

Jack certainly would. "He doesn't approve of the French, I'm afraid; and he certainly won't like the fact that my wife has been working as a weaver."

Ben had already decided that that was even more reason to ensure her hands became white and smooth and soft. Suzanne already behaved and spoke like the lady she was. If she looked like a great lady, too—dress, and jewels, and soft white skin—it was possible that the old man would never have to find out what she had had to do to survive. It was, Ben persuaded himself, by far the simplest solution.

Suzanne surprised him by laughing. "I'm not afraid of one grumpy old man, Ben, even if he is your grandfather. I'm not afraid of anything when we're together."

Ben swallowed hard. What a declaration. And in front of Dominic and Jack, too.

Suzanne had not finished. "We have faced danger and death together. We can face anything. Besides, we have our valiant friends to guard our backs." She smiled first at Jack and then at Dominic. "How can we possibly fail?"

Ben's reply was going to be much too intimate for present company. For the moment, he limited his reaction to a smile and a nod. Then he rose and offered a hand to her. "Shall we take a stroll, my love? These…um…*valiant friends* are nowhere near ready to leave. We have plenty of time to…um…enjoy the scenery."

Jack gave a snort of laughter which he turned into an unconvincing cough.

Dominic shot a sideways glance at Ben, but said only, "As you wish. Don't go beyond Leo's pickets."

Ben nodded and tucked Suzanne's hand into his arm. She even had a parasol, he was delighted to see. The newly-cosseted Lady Dexter should certainly be protecting her complexion. The moment they were out of sight of the others, Ben took her into his arms and kissed her, very very thoroughly. "Together, we cannot fail," he whispered into her hair. "Thank you, my love. For everything."

Some minutes later, they were ambling through a stand of umbrella pines to more open hillside beyond. There, they stood together, arm in arm, taking in the view. Below them, the lower slopes were covered with dense dark-leaved shrubs, dotted here and there with small trees. The ribbon of the road wound its way dustily between them and lost itself among the pines by the summit. Everywhere around them was hot and heavy and noisy with cicadas.

"It makes no sense," Ben began, puzzled. "I feel as if I recognise this place, but that's impossible. I've never been in this part of France before."

"Perhaps you saw other hillsides, further south, after you landed? I suppose one barren hillside is much like another."

"It's not barren," he said at once, drinking in the scent of wild herbs. There was rosemary here, and thyme. And was that lavender, too? He closed his eyes for a second. Yes, wonderfully soothing.

Here in the clearing, the turf was temptingly dry and springy underfoot. Unable to resist, he lay down on his back and put one hand behind his head, gazing up at the burning sky. "Join me, love?" He reached up his free hand to her. "It's beautiful here. Not barren at all. Smell those herbs."

In seconds, she had thrown down her parasol and she was lying beside him, holding his hand once more. They lay together in silence, savouring the scented peace of the place. It was blissful.

"No, I couldn't have seen a hillside like this," he decided. "Not here in France. I was shot when we'd barely arrived in Marseilles."

"Then you must have dreamt it," Suzanne said immediately, in that practical French way he loved.

"Dreamt it? Oh... Why, what a clever woman you are. Yes, that's precisely what I did. When I was wounded and raving. There was a hot hillside, just like this. I lay on it. And there was the scent of herbs, just like this. I smelt them. And there were tufts of yellow mimosa flowers, just…" He looked up. There was a twisted mimosa tree behind them, but it had no flowers.

"The mimosa flowers in the spring," Suzanne said, quellingly. Then she caught her breath. "Oh, but it was spring when you first came to me," she added in a whisper, marvelling.

"And finally," Ben went on, very sure of his memories now, "there was the voice of an angel, who gave me back my sanity. The mimosa may be missing, but the angel's voice is still here. Stay with me, angel?"

"Always," she said, and melted into his arms for the kiss that would seal their promises to each other.

THE END

Historical Note

NAPOLEON BONAPARTE SAILED from Elba to land in France at 5 p.m. on Wednesday 1 March 1815. That began The Hundred Days. Travel was difficult at first, since Napoleon had chosen to scramble his army of about 1000 men across the mountains to avoid opposition. By the time Napoleon reached Lyons, however, resistance was crumbling and regiments were rallying to support their returning Emperor.

The historical events I have shown in *His Silken Seduction* happened much as I have described. In Lyons, the troops changed sides even before Napoleon arrived. Earlier in the day, the King's brother, who was supposed to lead the regiments against Napoleon, found himself being mocked on the parade ground. He gave up any thought of fighting and decamped to Paris. Napoleon entered Lyons in triumph. Unopposed.

Napoleon remained some days in Lyons, issuing decrees and summoning the parliament to Paris. He also summoned his wife and son back from Vienna—though, if you have read Leo's story, *His Reluctant Mistress*, you will know that that did not go quite according to plan.

The French King, Louis XVIII, did not remain in Paris to oppose Napoleon's return. He fled to Brussels on Sunday, 19 March 2015. The following day, Napoleon entered Paris in triumph, without a shot being fired. Even Marshal Ney—who had promised the King that he would bring Napoleon to Paris as a prisoner in an iron cage—had changed sides.

In Vienna, the Duchess of Courland arrived on Good Friday to give the assembled monarchs the news they would have been dreading. Their political squabbles ended. Within a day, a new Allied Coalition had been formed and the Duke of Wellington had been appointed commander-in-chief. By early April, Wellington was in Brussels to take command of the army.

Soon, it was over. Napoleon lost the battle of Waterloo—on 18 June 1815—though, as Wellington admitted, it was *a damned close-run thing*. By the middle of July, Napoleon was on a British ship bound for England, and later, for exile in St Helena. King Louis XVIII had been restored to the throne of France.

But Waterloo was not the end of the violence for the people of France. Paris was occupied, filled with foreign troops. The situation was dangerous, and volatile. The Parisians were ready to rise against the occupiers, and royalists were clamouring for blood. No one was safe, in Paris and other cities. Even royalists were attacked for failing to oppose Napoleon with sufficient vigour. Republicans and Bonapartists were ready to fight, too, since they felt they had nothing to lose. Many people died in revenge attacks as gangs went on the rampage in cities such as Marseilles and Toulon—and in the famous silk-weaving centre, Lyons.

Dear Reader: from Joanna

I hope you sighed with pleasure when Ben was finally reunited with his beloved wife, Suzanne. And if you've read all four books of the Aikenhead Honours, you will know that Dominic and Leo and Jack are all happily settled, too. The Honours have been disbanded and each member is now set to make a new life with the woman of his heart. Even the incorrigible Jack seems to have turned over a new leaf and, with the estate that Dominic is bestowing on him, he and Marguerite will be able to create an independent and fulfilling life together.

I'd like to ask a favour now, please. If you enjoyed *His Silken Seduction*, I'd be really grateful if you could leave a review at your usual online store or on your favourite reader website. Your review can help other readers to find and enjoy my books, too. *Thank you!*

One other request. I've done everything I can to ensure this ebook is free of errors, but even the best of proofreaders can miss things. If your eagle eye spots a mistake, please do let me know, via email to joanna@libertabooks.com so that I can correct whatever has gone wrong at my end.

In case you were wondering, the old Joanna Maitland website is no longer available. It directs visitors to my new website at libertabooks.com/joanna where you can find information about me and my books.

You can also find links to my published books at Books2Read.com/JoannaMaitland.

Competitions, Free Short Stories, Giveaways and More

For news, free stories, competitions and giveaways, and lots of fun stuff, please visit the multi-author website at Libertà Books (libertabooks.com) where readers and authors chat and laugh about books, films, history, costume, the craft of writing and much more. You can have your say on the weekly Sunday blog, or maybe write a love letter to a favourite novel.

Intrigued? Have a look and see whether you would like to join in. You'd be most welcome. We often host writers you will know and we talk about all sorts of books which probably include many of your favourites.

The Libertà hive tweets on X @LibertaBooks and posts at FaceBook/libertabooks.

And, from 2025 on, you can find me on Blue Sky @joannamaitland.bsky.social too.

Unsuitable Matches Series

*A penniless runaway, a disfigured veteran and a cynical
rake — can such unsuitable matches ever succeed?*

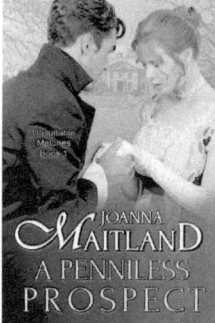 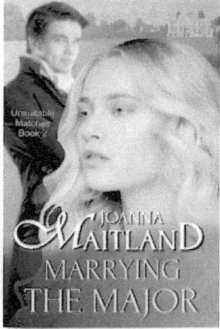 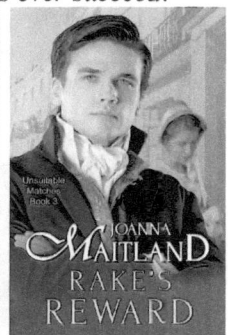

A Penniless Prospect

Dressed as a boy, Jessamyne, a plain and penniless young
lady, escapes a forced marriage to a vile old man. But can
she trust the masterful Earl Hardinge who
rescues her on the road?

Jessamyne—Jamie to those who love her—desperately
needs to stay hidden until she turns 21. Can her disguise as
a gardener's boy keep her safe on Richard's estate
until then? And will Richard betray Jamie to her vindictive
stepmother if he penetrates her disguise?

Marrying the Major

Heiress Emma Fitzwilliam remembers Hugo Stratton as a
handsome young officer with a wicked sense of humour.
But the Major Stratton who returns from the wars is a
scarred and prickly recluse who rebuffs all Emma's
attempts to get near him.

When Emma is threatened with ruin, marriage is the only
way to save her reputation. She longs to have Hugo
as her bridegroom, but will he propose to
a woman in disgrace?

And, even if he does, could a marriage between them ever
be made to work?

Rake's Reward

Marina Beaumont expects to become the demure
companion to Lady Luce, a reclusive old lady in her
declining years. But after five years in exile in Vienna, Kit
Stratton is back in London, bent on taking his revenge on
Marina's employer, the old harridan who caused his
disgrace and banishment.

When Lady Luce loses a fortune to Kit Stratton, Marina
expects to be packed off home, without a penny of the
wages her impoverished family desperately needs. So,
scandalous though it is, she must
beg Kit Stratton not to claim the debt.

What reward will a notorious rake demand in return for
Lady Luce's debt of honour?

Don't miss out!

Visit the website below and you can sign up to receive emails whenever Joanna Maitland publishes a new book. There's no charge and no obligation.

https://books2read.com/r/B-A-NPDLD-OGFJG

Connecting independent readers to independent writers.